T0067104

It's all Greek to me

It's all Greek to me

The tribulations and "trials" of life in
the field of Legal Interpreting!

KEITH AND ANGELIKY GARD

IT'S ALL GREEK TO ME
THE TRIBULATIONS AND "TRIALS" OF LIFE IN
THE FIELD OF LEGAL INTERPRETING!

iUniverse books may be ordered through booksellers or by contacting:

iUniverse
1663 Liberty Drive
Bloomington, IN 47403
www.iuniverse.com
1-800-Authors (1-800-288-4677)

Because of the dynamic nature of the Internet, any web addresses or links contained in this book may have changed since publication and may no longer be valid. The views expressed in this work are solely those of the author and do not necessarily reflect the views of the publisher, and the publisher hereby disclaims any responsibility for them.

Any people depicted in stock imagery provided by Thinkstock are models, and such images are being used for illustrative purposes only.
Certain stock imagery © Thinkstock.

ISBN: 978-1-4917-5637-9 (sc)
ISBN: 978-1-4917-5638-6 (e)

Print information available on the last page.

iUniverse rev. date: 01/12/2015

Contents

An ode to those that are gone, but not forgotten. You will always be loved and forever, we will be one family, for all eternity.

"What makes a superhero?"

This had been the question that for some reason has been repeatedly entering my thoughts.

It has been 6 moths since we lost my beautiful Father in January of 2014.

The connection between that and the passing of my Father baffled me.

Nobody understands the pain in losing a parent and sadly, no one can guide you as to when the pain finally subsides. Some days, that can be the hardest thing to understand and deal with when going through the everyday motions of living.

In times of sadness, depression and anxiety, my mind always wondered back to the exploits of those on the big screen.

It wasn't until that I had reached my "rock bottom" that the connection between that random thought and the devastating life loss, became abundantly clear.

My Father is the true definition of a superhero. An ordinary person wanting to complete extraordinary good deeds, in the society we live in.

They were put into situations that were hard, tough and challenging, yet stuck "by their guns" to face the world head on.

They knew what was right and what was wrong.

They cared for and loved those closest to them.

They always offered support to those in need, sometimes anonymously, without wanting anything in return.

So for the first time in my life, as a direct result of my passion for anything film, I realised, superheroes are like my beautiful father, and that they are all around us every day. We just don't know it.

It sometimes takes a loss, sadly, to come to this realisation.

So the next time you have the fortunate opportunity to go and see the latest blockbuster on the big screen, of course marvel at their heroics and accomplishments. Cheer when they defeat the bad guy and smile when they fly into the victorious sunset.

Like the heroes on the silver screen that dazzle us with their "Herculean" feats of strength, we will always know that our Fathers legacy will live on through the love he has for us that has subsequently shaped our lives and through the next generation of grandkids/"little heroes" who are slowly readying themselves to take on the ever changing "new world order".

So like the light in the night sky that signals a certain heroes call to action, the light of our Fathers love will always shine in our lives. Guiding us to remember where we have come from, giving us direction as to where we are going but also, letting us never forget what a beautiful person we had, that touched our heart.

Thank you for buying Mum and Dads book and supporting his legacy. I can just picture him now, knowing how happy he would be with the thought of people getting so much joy, laughter and pleasure from this book. Something that was 10 years in the making , but full of a lifetimes memories.

A legacy, like that of a hero, we will always honour and whose presence on this earth for 75 years, we will never forget.

He will always be apart of us through the movie of our lives, a movie that we call life.

Andrew C. Gard
London. July 2014.

Prologue

Keith and I decided it was about time to leave home and revisit Greece, the place we met, revisit old friends and places from the days of our youth. The family in Athens were always asking us to return – making plans as to where they would take us.

The big day arrived – so early on a freezing wet August morning we piled into a taxi bus and rocketed off to Melbourne Airport. We vowed and declared that the driver was an out of work "Formula 1" participant – we were there so quickly for there was a long journey ahead.

The new "Eleftherios Veniselos" Airport built just prior to the Athens Olympic Games was a revelation – all polished marble, stainless steel and a train that entered the passenger terminal.

After Customs & Immigration formalities - we were free.

Although in the early hours of the morning "the family" were there and waiting to welcome us. So our holiday began – long days of "catching up" and of course plenty of day excursions.

One such was to the first Greek Air Show entitled "Archangelos 2005", held at the Air force airport at Tanagra, set in the rolling farmlands one hour by rail outside Athens.

We left early one morning – electing to travel by rail, as the roads would have been almost impossible.

The journey by super efficient "Metro" was fast and comfortable. After a short journey we transferred to the intrastate station in downtown Athens, and waited for the train to Tanagra.

Finally, after a wait of some 45 minutes, it rolled into the platform.

As luck would have it, a carriage doorway presented itself directly in front of my husband and I, so to avoid being crushed by the throng I grabbed Keith and we jumped aboard.

My brother in law Nick was not so lucky when he tried to follow us.

Being a man of considerable stature, he became wedged in the carriage doorway, with the head of stout little lady in black stuck under his arm.

Why — because she was determined to be the first inside − "come what may".

Neither of them could move. The more she pushed the tighter they became wedged.

The crowd, becoming impatient at being kept waiting pushed even harder. Then panic set in.

The screaming from the lady in black was deafening. A stalemate developed during which our stout little lady in black lost her footing, stocking feet waving in the breeze, her head was still firmly wedged under Nicks arm.

My husband Keith had no idea what the commotion was all about, until understanding what was happening, I ran to the doorway calling on the crowd to fall back, while I tried to extricate the trapped couple

The following is a rough translation of the words screamed by a very upset and disheveled, stout little lady in black.

'Who do you think you are — you nearly killed me,' she screamed.

Nick responded with, 'madam if you had not pushed so hard to get in front of me, this would never have occurred.'

Not to be silenced she ranted — 'but I was trying to be the first person inside.'

Then I knew I was back in Greece!

Nick shrugged his shoulders and tried to ignore her.

So off we went to the airport at Tanagra – what a day it proved for Keith & Nick - aircraft from all over the world were put through their paces.

The same could not be said for my sister Jenny and I – for when the temperature reached 44C we persuaded Nick and Keith to have lunch at a Taverna under the spreading branches of an old plane tree. A least it was cool.

Much later we arrived home tired but refreshed and relaxed, for the following day we were to attend a wedding on a beautiful Greek island – which formed part of Western Greece.

Our friends Sophia and Costa were to be married on the lovely little Ionian island of Lefkas – Greece.

I was invited to act as their "Koubara" or (Matron of Honor). We were both surprised and delighted as it would give us the opportunity to revisit this most beautiful region of Greece once again.

Set like a jewel in calm turquoise waters of the west coast, it forms a natural "stepping stone" to other Ionian islands which of course include the picturesque island of Scorpios - playground of the Greek tycoon Aristotle Onassis.

Some years ago Keith and I enjoyed some golden days in the sun when we holidayed in this delightful part of Greece - it was a magic location and we knew it would be an ideal place to celebrate our friend's wedding.

Since arriving in Australia and my initial foray into the world of banking, Sophia and her "husband to be" Costa became our close personal friends – naturally we were delighted to take part. in the celebration of their special day.

Our Nihon aircraft departed Athens "Eleftherios Veniselos" airport, climbing up over the reclaimed olive tree groves heading west bound for the recently refurbished airport at Preveza, which is only a 30 minute taxi ride from our destination - the town of Lefkas.

A cup of thick sweet Greek coffee later, we swooped low over the sparkling blue of the Ionian, prior to hearing a satisfying "clunk" as the undercarriage of our little aircraft locked into place prior to landing.

Being an aircraft intended for domestic and inter-island use, the retrieval of our luggage was a relatively easy matter, after which we set off by taxi for the town of Lefkas.

Lefkas can be described as an island by default and is the only one linked to mainland Greece by a swing bridge, giving it easy access by road. As you approach the bridge, lining the banks of the canal are muzzle loading cannons, their barrels set vertically to serve as bollards for the yachts which call there during the summer months.

Owing to the large number of guests attending, not only from other parts of Greece, but from other European countries and beyond - accommodation was at a premium. We counted ourselves lucky to have secured accommodation at the Hotel Lefkas situated on the waterfront which enjoyed an unparalleled view of the harbor and town.

Since its inception, Lefkas had enforced town planning laws that ensured the maximum height of buildings in the town (2 floors) was not exceeded thus preserving its architectural integrity.

Our accommodation at the Hotel Lefkas stretched along the edge of the harbor blending in harmoniously with the waterfront.

It was here in the hotel we had arranged to meet the other members of the wedding party.

Firstly there was Ross – a tall bright gregarious Australian with his wife Cleo, a colleague from my banking days – both close friends of Costa and Sophis.

Next was Jim, a member of Costa's football team.

It was his wife Toni who was instrumental in teaching Sophia English some years ago and into the bargain she introduced her to Costa – another student of her English class.

Last but not least was Arthur – the only one of our group who remained unmarried.

He was a clerk working for the Passport Office, who met the couple originally as a result of assisting them with their Passport Applications.

So there you have a picture of our wedding party.

Oh before I forget – naturally it also included Keith and I.

Tradition dictates that on the last night of his "bachelorhood", his male friends take the groom out for his last "night on the town".

That night was no exception; so Keith and "the boys" pooled their resources to ensure he had an experience to remember.

It's fair to say that they achieved their goal for as it was an experience he won't forget in a hurry!

What happened you might ask – well suffice to say that the "Taverna of the Seven Brothers" will long remember the antics of those rowdy Australians men that night - so far from their home. Needless to say they paid dearly with their sore heads on the next day.

The following morning, we were awakened by an out of tune "cacophony of sound" from the local brass band as it marched up and down the quay outside, manfully trying to render a version of some of Sousa's marches. After a night on the town, the noise the noise they made was a shattering experience for the "boys"!

After a light breakfast, we left by taxi from the hotel for the quay at Nidri – to do a little prearranged fishing.

Upon our arrival, and boarding a boat (which it appeared had seen better days), the motor reluctantly coughing into life, and we set off across a calm "wine dark sea" in a scene reminiscent of a verse from one of the great Lord Byron's poems.

According to the fisherman, in order to reach the optimum location to catch fish, it was best to head south to an area between the beautiful green pine tree clad slopes of Skorpios, (still the island property of the Greek tycoon Aristotle Onassis's family) and the island of Meganissi - legendary home of Jason.

Meganissi's other claim to fame is the cave that sheltered the only Greek submarine the "Papanikolis", throughout almost all of the German occupation during the second World War

The hiding place of "Papanikolis" was the second largest sea cave in Greece. It is not a pure sea cave but a "karst cave" fed by fresh water as well as being partly flooded by the sea.

Located on the south coast of the island, the cave consists of a huge central chamber formed a fully protected natural harbor. It's the size of a medium indoor sports hall covering 3800 square meters, and has been used over the ages, as a refuge by ships endangered by violent weather. It is large enough to even accommodate sailing ships with their tall masts and sails. During the 2nd World War it was the "lair" of the renegade Hellenic Navy submarine "Papanikolis" after which the cave has been named.

The German sea patrols searched in vain – for it remained undiscovered until the end of the Second World War.

Eventually, forced to flee its home, it spent the rest of the War dodging the German battle fleet.

The water was calm and crystal clear. Large schools of fish flashed past as we stopped to make ready the lines – suddenly there was a hiss and shower of water as a pod of dolphins played around the boat. Naturally this caused us to sit up and watch. Our initial reaction was to identify them as sharks was incorrect - they would have been so out of place in such an idyllic setting.

The sea view and the beautiful combination of the different green and blue shades of color left us speechless as we drank in the wonder of the seascape.

Time however marched on and the fishing only moderately successful, so a discussion ensued as to what to do next, while the "skipper" served small cups of sweet dark Greek coffee and biscuits.

Scorpios was visible in the distance, so it was decided to cruise to the island and if possible circumnavigate it. The island was made famous some years ago by the later day exploits of Jacqueline Kennedy/ Onassis and opera diva Maria Callas.

The island proved to be a place of exquisite natural beauty – peaceful golden sandy beaches, and a forest of pine trees protecting terraced flower gardens stretching down to the waters edge.

Rounding the next headland we were greeted by the sight of Nidri slumbering in the early afternoon sunshine.

Conscious of the time, we decided to return to the hotel in Lefkas to change for the ceremony later in the afternoon.

If only they'd known what was about to transpire!

Setting off for Nidri; the sea was calm and the weather pleasantly warm.

Suddenly there was a violent scraping sound and a lurch as the boat shuddered to a jarring halt. The excursion had been so smooth and trouble free to that point – unfortunately our luck was about to change!

The "skipper" had misjudged the tide, and we were aground on a sand bar between Island of Scorpios and the harbor at Nidri.

Under normal circumstances we would have reached for the fishing lines – but in this case our party had a date to attend Costa's wedding, in which we all had a part.

The "skipper" looked worried – very worried as he put the boat's motor into reverse to back off the sand bar – to no avail. The sand swirled clouding the water as the motor screamed and the boat shuddered – it was stuck fast!

A solution had to be found and quickly – the time was ticking away and worse - the groom was starting to panic!

Keith jumped overboard wearing a face mask, surveyed the scene confirming that we were aground on a sand bar near the entrance to Nidri harbor.

They tried rocking the boat to and fro, also entering the water while our skipper reversed the motor once again – all to no avail.

Panic started to set in, when a fishing boat observing our predicament drew alongside, throwing us a line – eventually, after a deal of pulling, the boat was free.

'Head for Nidri quickly or I will be late for my own wedding', Spiro called to the "skipper". The boat commenced to pick up speed as it headed for Nidri harbor.

Meanwhile – understanding the urgency, the "skipper" used his mobile phone to awaken one of his taxi driver friends requesting a car to meet the boat and take his passengers to Lefkas town.

Finally arriving at the stone jetty they leaped into an ancient taxi, after paying the fisherman the agreed amount for the use of his boat.

Time was against them however, as they rocketed up the east side of the island towards Lefkas - suddenly there was a loud "bang" and the taxi lurched to a halt in a cloud of dust.

We'd had a "blow out" – now this really spelt trouble, as our time line was becoming really tight. Out they piled as the taxi driver searched around the back of the taxi for his spare. Fortunately the car was an ancient Holden which by "fair means or foul" had found its way to Lefkas. This meant they were familiar as to where the "spare" could be located.

In record time the spare wheel had been fitted and we were on our way.

Costa was really worried as they rounded a corner into the town and drove up to the front of the hotel, paying the smiling driver who declared that it was the first time his passengers had done the dirty work!

At that stage, as time was critical, they asked the driver to wait while we changed - a taxi was a rare sight at that time of day and they had to travel to the wedding.

In Greece, between the hours of 1pm to 5pm it's "siesta time". Shops and offices close as workers go home for the afternoon nap. The streets are deserted except for the odd donkey or stray dog wandering around. It's not so widely practiced these days in the major cities.

On Lefkas, *everyone* observed the custom.

Mindful of this, Spiro ensured at least we had transport.

'Okay folks, he said. The drive up the mountain should take us about 25 minutes going by my previous experience. Now as we have an hour's leeway, let's meet in the foyer in say 30 minutes at 4.30 pm'.

The last we saw of the taxi driver, was him settling back to wait for us under a plane tree, his black "Zorba" hat pulled down to over his eyes, as he commenced to catch up on some "shut eye".

Upstairs, everyone showered, shaved and changed.

Outside, the town slumbered in the full heat of a summer's afternoon, interrupted only by the shrill scream of millions of cicada's who appeared to be enjoying the solitude brought on by the temperature.

Exactly 30 minutes later, we were ready, meeting together in the hotels foyer. 'Okay we are all present said Spiro — let's go for the taxi before some other drama occurs.'

Outside as the reflected heat shimmered up from the road - there was no sign of the taxi or its driver - they had vanished!

The groom turned ashen – 'what will we do, he cried. How can we travel up to the church, we have only 10 minutes before the ceremony is due to start. The taxi drivers are all asleep or at home!'

Suddenly, a white and blue police van pulled up in a cloud of dust. Its occupant had observed a group of formally dressed people wandering around, one of whom was wringing his hands in despair.

'What will we do – oh *what* will we do - Costa cried!'

The policeman left his van and walked across the road to investigate the disturbance.

Saluting briskly he confined his remarks to Costa in Greek.

'Hey my friends, you all seem very uptight – what is the problem, perhaps I can help you' he enquired.

Not considering that the policeman's approach was anything other than a professional one – Costa poured out our sorry tale.

Peering from behind his big black sunglasses the officer observed. 'Oh your getting married – now when and what is the name of the village and church.'

Costa gave him a short description of the location and name of the church.

The policeman responded – 'at this time of day it's impossible to engage a taxi. Now you don't have to do this, but if you wish I would be pleased to drive you and your friends up to the village in my police van.

I'll get you to the church on time!'

Costa turned to us saying, 'the kind officer has offered to give us a lift up to the church – let's go.'

We were surprised, travel to the wedding in a police van – but the circumstances were such that we were desperate.

Boarding the van, the door slammed shut — we roared up the mountain road, siren wailing as the driver cleared the odd donkey and herd of sheep out of the way.

So Costa and Sophia were married according to the Byzantine rites of the Greek Orthodox Church – and did they live happily ever after?

Of course they did – but that's another story!

Chapter 1

"The Romeo of Gore Street"

The advertisement said interpreters were required by Frank Manier and Associates of Richmond, there was a phone number so I telephoned and made an appointment.

Mr Manier proved to be a jovial middle aged gentleman of European origin who managed an interpreting agency and taxation consultancy.

Almost every nationality was catered for.

He showed me into his office, took my particulars, and expressed delight when he heard I had been employed as a Greek interpreter by the English, Scottish &Australian Bank.

Sighing deeply he opened a large leather bound diary and began:

'Well, Mrs Gard, we'll throw you in at the deep end first. I propose to send you to your first court case on Wednesday morning at Coburg Magistrates Court in Bell Street.

You are to report to a John Ambrose who is appearing on behalf of a Katina Papadopoulos.

I believe it's some sort of marital problem - it's important to ensure you're there by 9.30am as court starts at 10am. Here's a copy of our salary rates,' he said, handing them to me.

With that we shook hands, and my career as a freelance Greek interpreter commenced.

The next day following a sleepless night, I left home having to stop my car part way to consult my street directory to find the Coburg court house. I arrived in an absolute mental panic. The weather was freezing. A bitterly cold wind howled down Bell Street, as I tried to find a lady of Greek appearance outside.

The street was deserted - where was everyone?

I walked up and down outside. Oh, why had I decided to come to this strange place!

Where are the beaches of Vouliagmeni and the warm Mediterranean sunshine I knew so well.

Before freezing completely, I decided to enter the building.

There she was in the foyer, a large lady in black talking to a tall, pinched, balding, bespectacled gentleman clutching a pile of papers bound in pink tape.

I had found my first client.

Had I known what was to follow, it would have taken a team of wild horses to drag me into that courtroom.

I introduced myself to a Mr Ambrose, and then faced my client — a symphony in black.

Obviously relieved, she burst into a torrent of Greek divulging some of the most intimate details of her married life — leaving poor Ambrose floundering in her wake.

Thankfully she finally ran out of steam.

'Well, Mrs Gard, - after all that I hope you know what the problem is,' remarked Ambrose.

'Yes, I replied, she has told me everything, absolutely everything' – I started to worry.

The lady had problems, big problems. My legs turned to jelly; how was I going to divulge her bed room secrets in public? The details were **very** embarrassing.

The more I tried to calm her, the more she remonstrated with me.

Judging by his puzzled expression it showed, Ambrose had not the slightest idea as what was being said. The problem was extremely personal. Apparently her husband was neglecting her wishes in bed. To make matters worse she had caught him in a compromising position with other women.

'Mr Ambrose, I wonder could we discuss her problem in a less public place,' I suggested.

He ushered us into a private conference room – I think he had a suspicion about what was coming.

Wishing the earth would swallow me, I briefly told him of her sorry tale.

Much to my surprise, he did not appear unduly fazed, saying, 'tell her to keep her answers brief and please instruct her not answer my questions with a question, and bore the court with a lot of extraneous detail.' - I did as he requested.

Now came the boring part, we had to wait and wait to be called.

A small crowd thronged the entrance to the courtroom, coughing nervously while puffing on foul smelling cigarettes, but the wind continued to howl outside.

And so the time passed.

Periodically a sleepy faced clerk emerged from the warmth of the courtroom to request the next sets of combatants follow him.

Eventually a nasal booming voice thundered out, 'Papadopoulos. V. Papadopoulos.'- my moment of truth was at hand. We entered the oak paneled court room, which initially felt slightly warmer than the arctic conditions outside. Seated high above us in all his glory was magistrate Fortiscue, a stout florid faced man bundled up in a thick overcoat and scarf, obviously suffering from a severe cold.

I sat with Mrs. Papadopoulos waiting nervously, while Ambrose cleared his throat and commenced. 'Your Worship I appear for the plaintiff, Katina Papadopoulos.'

Magistrate Fortiscue continued to write without raising his head. 'Yes, thank you, and who appears for the husband?' he replied without looking up.

The silence was deafening, the magistrate stopped writing, raised his head peering peering over the top half of his glasses in order to see why there was no reaction from the husband's counsel. It was left to Mr. Ambrose to inform the magistrate there was no one appearing for the husband.

'Oh, all right, we will deal with the wife first', the magistrate growled.

'Kindly state your name, address, and occupation', requested the clerk of courts.

I sprang into action interpreting exactly what was being said. Before I finished Mrs Papadopoulos replied 'Katina Papadopoulos of 6, Gore Street Fitzroy,' in English.

She paused looking around nervously; (come on Katina there's more) I thought mentally prompting her. Then she turned to me with a fierce expression on her face shouting in half Greek and English - 'why he wants to know my job?'

Not wishing to interrupt the flow, I translated 'home duties your worship.' Katina turned to me saying in Greek, 'ask him why he wants to know about my job'— referring to the magistrate. I instinctively held her arm trying to stop further remarks as Ambrose arose to speak. So far so good, I thought.

Mr. Ambrose proceeded to shuffle his pile of papers and finding the correct piece, he commenced. 'Your worship, my client came to this country some twenty years ago, she was married and subsequently divorced, having an eighteen year old daughter from her first marriage. Twelve months ago she returned to her birthplace, a small village in southern Greece, for a holiday. It was there she met and subsequently married John Papadopoulos.

I present a copy of the Marriage Certificate, which I will ask our interpreter to translate in order to confirm its authenticity.'

A rather crumpled document was handed to me. I read the contents complete with official rubber stamp impressions and appropriate stamp duty. I confirmed that it was genuine document, handing it back to Ambrose.

To my right, Katina puffed and snorted her impatience. It was then I realized that she was after blood, thankfully not mine but her husband's.

The clerk of courts yawned, no doubt contemplating the nice warm cup of tea awaiting him during the recess.

The magistrate scribbled onwards, seemingly oblivious of the simmering volcano rumbling to his left.

Katina commenced – she had first realized the problem after receiving a complete lack of his attention in the marital bed.

After a great deal of soul searching she followed him one fine summer's evening to discover that instead of attending the Pan Hellenic Social Club he had proceeded to a more amorous rendezvous.

Mr Papadopoulos, realizing her frustration was bubbling to the surface, glanced around furtively, no doubt seeking the best avenue down which to beat a hasty retreat — finally it happened.

Suspicious that not all of her testimony had been interpreted, all 152 cm of Katina exploded, for she decided to help herself. 'No f.... ing business judge, no sex,' she bellowed in English, glowering at her husband who had visibly shrunk in his seat.

The previously disinterested magistrate's head jerked upwards — glasses flew from his nose clattering to the floor below. The clerk of courts awoke from his stupor and rushed to rescue them. Spectators in the body of the court dissolved into laughter. This caused the magistrate to glower at me growling, 'madam interpreter control your client.'

I proceeded to admonish Katina telling her another outburst like that and she was really in trouble. The magistrate, red faced and very angry requested the clerk to restore order or he said the Court would be cleared.

The observers in the body of the court were starting to enjoy themselves. They settled down in anticipation of Round 2. Magistrate Fortescue invited John Padopoulos to climb up into the witness box. There was no reaction. Realizing that his English was limited, I asked the magistrate if I could help the situation. Magistrate Fortescue appeared relieved, visibly softening his attitude towards me.

'If you would be so kind,' he cooed.

Concluding Katina's evidence, the magistrate dismissed her from the witness box.

So having gained the magistrates permission I invited her husband to join me.

Dressed in a black crumpled suit, white shirt and black pointed shoes, he squeaked across the room from his seat, joining me in the witness box.

Occasionally he glanced furtively in his wife's direction.

'Madam interpreter, would you be kind enough to assist by explaining the oath to the defendant.'

'Yes your worship,' I replied and commenced to explain the contents of the little plastic laminated card.

Then the questioning commenced.

Apparently Australia was the big adventure in John's life. When Katina arrived in his village on holiday, he was swept off his feet by this amorous lady. The prospect of leaving the goats, sheep and his village behind, and traveling to "the Big Country" was too much — Katina proposed and he accepted.

Life had changed for John and the temptations of the flesh in the big city particularly female ones, proved too much for him.

Katina first realized the problem after receiving a complete lack of attention in the marital bed. In other words – ignoring Katina's wants, he simply turned over and went to sleep!

After a great deal of soul searching, she decided to follow him one fine summers evening to discover that instead of attending the Pan Hellenic Social Club, he had proceeded to an amorous rendezvous.

In other words he was "cheating" on her.

In the body of the court, Katina chafed with impatience she wanted justice —and poor John was only too aware of this as he glanced nervously in her direction.

Eventually after it appeared he had worn out his pen, magistrate Fortescue stopped peering over the rim of his glasses and focused on Ambrose.

"In light of the extremely agitated state of your client, I think it advisable at this stage if I adjoun this matter to another day and time.'

'If your Worship pleases,' Ambrose replied with a shrug of his shoulders.

The change of plans had to be translated to Katina − this was the part I was dreading.

'Mrs Papadopoulos, I commenced in Greek, the magistrate has decided that he will not proceed any further and that a decision will be made at a later date.

Mr Ambrose will be in contact with you.'

Katina snorted in fury for she considered that John had erred and should be punished.

In her mind the legal system had failed, John was getting off "scot" free.

Men being men, the magistrate and barristers were on his side.

Drawing herself up to her full height, she decided that as the legal system had failed, she would personally ensure John did not get off lightly, 'crookithes, crookithes,(crooks) she trumpeted, 'alle crookithes.'

She meant of course that the magistrate had been bribed, the barrister had been bribed, in fact the only person to escape her wrath was me, so I stepped aside to let her calm down.

Looking around, I noticed that the magistrate, accompanied by the clerk of courts beating a 'hasty retreat', both disappearing into the chambers at the rear of the court, no doubt intent on seeking solace in a quiet cup of morning tea. Without warning Katina stood there snorting with fury, seizing her husband by the collar and commenced to beat him over the head with the handle of her black umbrella.

Ambrose dropped his files, and assisted by the court usher, they separated the struggling pair, who were rolling around on the floor at that stage.

Freed from her clutches, John bolted for the front door, and the last I saw of them, was Katina wailing like a "banshee" and chasing John down Bell St. Coburg - attempting to beat him with the "business end" of her black umbrella.

'Had a good day in court; how did the first case go?' my husband ventured when I arrived home looking as white as a sheet.

'I had one of the worst experiences of my life, just look at my face', I replied If you think I'll enter a Court again you're mistaken — I'm going to quit,' I raged.

But quit I didn't.

There were many other cases — subsequent changes to the Matrimonial Law Act have made the question of divorce far more civilized - *thank goodness!*

Chapter 2

"A favour for the Godmother"

Judge Griffith was "grumpy" on a Monday morning — today was no exception.

Firstly his car would not start, and Mrs Griffith had insisted that he wheel out the rubbish bin in front of their Lansell Road Toorak property before leaving. This was one of his major weekly irritations. He was unused to having to perform such menial tasks, being pandered to five days a week by his associate and clerk. To add to this irritation, upon his arrival, another vehicle occupied his parking space in the Supreme Court car park.

'Fellows, he roared, at a green coated parking attendant — who the blazes has parked this "bucket of bolts" in my spot?'

'Sorry your Honor,' replied the attendant who scurried out and took the judge's keys.

'I'll ensure the Holden is moved immediately and the "Roller" is parked in its correct position – it was one of the new barristers. He left before I could find him a spot.'

'Hamm, the judge replied clearing his throat, what's was the blighter's name eh?'

Fellows reflected for a moment, 'I think his name was Taylor — that's right Andrew Taylor.'

Grabbing a large sheaf of legal papers from the rich cowhide passenger seat of his silver Rolls Royce, he slammed the door and set off across the cobbled courtyard to the judges' entrance. Once inside he headed for his chambers at the rear of court no 4 to be greeted by his clerk, a thin bearded young man — Ron Barnes.

'I have told you before Barnes shave off that apology of a beard, this place is not a mortuary, you look like an undertaker's assistant on his day off.'

'Yes your Honor,' replied his clerk, inclining his eyes toward the heavens as if seeking divine guidance.

Well, and what have we got on today?' he growled.

'Your Honor, it's a stabbing at the Whisky Au Go Go,' replied Barnes.

'The – a – what did you say?' mumbled the judge.

'Your Honor, it's a stabbing at the Whisky Au Go Go,' replied Barnes.

'What in heaven's name is that?' growled the judge demonstrating his naivety.

'Your Honor, it's an establishment one attends to drink alcoholic liquor to enjoy ones self — in other words a night club.'

'Oh hmm, thank you Barnes, presumably a place where one partakes of a whisky or two and after that it's all go go — eh, how say you Barnes?'

'Very droll your Honor,' remarked the poker faced clerk sensing an improvement in the judge's humor.

Having donned his wig and scarlet vestments, he bellowed, 'right Barnes lead on, let's get on with it, we're late already.'

He loved the pure theatrics of it. In he swept to "grace" the bench - wig, scarlet and ermine robes — the lot. It reminded him of his days in the university student theatre and his appearance in Gilbert & Sullivan's – "Trial by jury".

He nodded to the court tipstaff, who bellowed, 'be upstanding in court, the Honorable Judge Griffiths is presiding.' The body of the court rose as one bowing to "he" who sat on the throne. 'Surely this is better than those halcyon student days,' thought the judge, restraining himself from bursting into song.

The City of Melbourne, in particular the western end around Queen St, is an area housing a multitude of barristers in a rabbit warren known as Owen Dixon Chambers.

Here they dwell amid a clutter of musty legal papers and yards and yards of pink ribbon.

Owen Dixon Chambers is almost equidistant between the bland forties style architecture of the County Court, and the nineteen century Victorian edifice known as the Supreme Court – a colonial clone of London's Old Bailey. It was in these two buildings that I gained much of my experience — nothing daunts me now if I am face any difficult situations. Settlements are negotiated, hearts broken, and some "lucky people" can be invited on a holiday as a guest of Her Majesty.

There were a number of interpreters propelling themselves along those Victorian corridors of power. It was in such a hectic working environment I was introduced to a small group who habitually occupied an area in one of the coffee shops known as "Interpreters Corner". It provided a welcome respite from the law, clients and barristers who, if you were unfortunate enough to join them for lunch, would "bash your ears" about their problems, aches and pains. It proved to be the best place to learn the best legal gossip as to who had become divorced, separated or remarried.

Presiding over this hotbed of scandal and rumor was Lily, the Diva or Godmother.

She was an amply proportioned, immaculately dressed, impeccably groomed Greek Egyptian lady who was in constant demand by the legal fraternity on account of the numerous European and Middle Eastern languages she spoke.

Not only did she have impressive language skills, vast experience, and a sympathetic ear, but an encyclopedic knowledge benefiting newcomers such as myself..

Best of all, she was a lovely person and delighted to help anyone in trouble.

She greeted me one day with — 'Dahhling, I have the ideal opportunity for you to break into some of the more interesting cases. I am in court on an other case, and they have asked me to handle a matter in the Supreme Court on the same day — would you be able to help me?'

I was happy to agree.

Early the following morning I was consulting the notice board listing the cases for hearing in the Supreme Court. Yes, there it is — Court number 4 in the West Wing.

Glancing around I observed a bewigged gentleman in a flowing black gown standing next to a thick set grey haired gentleman obviously Greek.

13

KEITH AND ANGELIKY GARD

They looked toward me with questioning expressions.

'Excuse me, are you James Taylor?' I asked

'I'm your Greek interpreter Angeliky Gard.

The inhabitant of the gaunt black gown broke into a beaming smile. 'Yes indeed I am, he said turning to the grey haired man. 'This is Mr Douras, his English is limited. All I have to go on is his solicitor's version of events. Would you ask Mr Douras to relate his version of what happened? It's going to be an uphill battle to defend this one. I fear for it appears that he is very much to blame. He stabbed a woman and should go to jail for nine years — if he's lucky.'

This is something I could do without, I thought.

Facing Mr Douras, I asked him in Greek, 'please tell me what has happened?'

Thrusting his palms toward me in an expressive continental gesture he exclaimed, 'she hit me so I stabbed her.' Could it be that simple, I thought?

'Okay Mr Douras,' I said in Greek, please tell me the complete story so that Mr Taylor and I can try and help you.'

Running his hand through his thick grey/ black hair he poured out the story in a steady stream of Greek, with the occasional English word thrown in for good measure.

Apparently my client was a photographer in his spare time at the Whisky – Au – Go – Go in the suburb of St.Kilda. Situated on the foreshore, the nightclub could best be likened to a poor version of what you would expect to find in a seedy part of the Greek port of Piraeus.

This was worse, for its reputation was really bad.

His job involved walking from table to table taking his photographs, using an oversized flashlight equipped camera — usually much to the annoyance of most patrons.

On one such evening, he stopped at a table where a couple of local thugs were seated.

They appeared to have evil designs on a young copper haired hostess sitting between them.

'Can I take your photograph?' asked our hero.

'Go and get lost,' one of the two men growled.

Rather than do as they had suggested he raised and aimed his camera, the flashlight exploded with a flash of blinding white light.

That proved to be his big mistake.

Both gentlemen' grabbed our client (one by each arm, so he was helpless). The hostess split the corner of his mouth with a vicious right hook. The damage being caused by a large dress ring she was wearing. Tables were overturned, "bouncers" summonsed, and poor Costas ejected. Undaunted, he returned to the nightclub an hour later clutching a hunting knife.

Lurking in the background, he waited until the hostess arose to go to the toilet, then he confronted her before using the knife to stab her, lacerating one of her kidneys. The police were called, and our client arrested and charged — later to be bailed by a friend.

I interpreted this sorry tale to Mr. Taylor, who looked more and more despondent; interspersing my story with —'Oh dear, Oh dear.' Suddenly the corridor outside burst into life when a huge red nosed Clerk of Courts bellowed - 'The Crown V Douras' and we took our seats at the front of the courtroom.

'Who do we have appearing for the plaintiff?' inquired the judge. 'I am your Honor,' exclaimed our barrister.

'What is your name sir?' asked the Judge. 'Andrew Taylor, your Honor'- was his response.

'Aaarump, you're the gentleman who needs some parking lessons,' observed the Judge.

'I'm sorry your Honor, stammered a confused Andrew Taylor, peering at the Judge, I don't understand.'

'Oh, never mind Taylor, just get on with it, the Judge growled, and who is prosecuting?'

'I am your Honor, my name is Stanley Brown, I'm appearing for the Crown,' said a tall gentleman who had the physical appearance of an ex- policeman.

Suddenly Judge Griffith realized to his dismay that the collar stud which had been giving trouble, slipped and the cravat which was neatly in place under his chin had started to droop.

He hastily placed his hand to his throat to ensure that the item was back in place.

'Your Honor, on the 16th of September this year, a Greek gentleman, namely the defendant Constantine Douras, was involved in an altercation at the Whisky Au Go Go of St Kilda. It is alleged that the aggrieved — Maria Polanski suffered severe lacerations.

The defendant has therefore been charged with causing grievous bodily harm, which I will seek to prove.'

'Mr Taylor, would you be kind enough to open the case for the defense,' the Judge growled without looking up from his writing.

'Your Honor, it is the defense's intention to demonstrate, that as a result of the extreme provocation suffered by my client, it was his natural reaction to defend himself as best he could when threatened by the associates of Ms Polinski.'

'Mr Taylor, said the judge, 'according to the charge sheets, it was not so much a case of defending himself but that of revenge, which puts the whole matter in a very different light.'

My legs shook, as the judge said, 'madam interpreter, please enter the witness box and take the oath.'

I did as he requested, then turning to my client, who had been invited to join me, handed him the Bible and saying in Greek, 'would you raise your right hand and repeat after me.' My client froze, beads of perspiration broke out on his forehead.

The judge — realizing that Constantine had a bad case of stage fright, interrupted the proceedings. 'Madam interpreter, can the tipstaff bring your client a glass of water?'

'Yes, thank you, your Honor,' I replied.

After gulping down the water, Constantine repeated the oath, and we were over the first hurdle.

'Mr Taylor, would you be kind enough to examine your client,' requested the judge peering over the rim of his glasses, trying to focus on my nervous colleague who was vainly searching through his notes.

'Your Honor, by cross examining my client I will show that his action was one of self defense. He was being attacked by three people and was in fear of his life. Mr Douras is a family man, he has never been in trouble with the law and was working as a photographer, when he became involved in this most unfortunate affair. His reaction in raising the knife was to protect himself. It was regrettable that Ms Polinski chose that moment to thrust herself at my client causing the wound.'

Valiant I thought, but not nearly good enough!

'Your Honor,' he cotinued facing to the Judge, 'my client is not a thug. He came to Australia, not to escape anything, but for a new life. He is married and has two children.

He is a hard worker on the production line of the Dunlop Factory at Broadmeadows.

He works as a photographer on a part time basis — using the extra money to support his wife who is seriously ill with a spinal complaint.'

'Hmm,' rumbled the Judge looking at the jury; 'it's known as "Mediterranean Back", a very painful malady ladies and gentlemen of the jury, not uncommon to people from his country. How say you, Taylor?'

'That is true your Honor,' replied my colleague, thankful for the interruption.

'Mrs Gard, would you ask Mr Douras to give his version of the events that led to the incident,' requested the Judge.

Constantine proceeded to give his own version while the Judge scribbled furiously, wrinkling his nose from time to time to adjust the focal length of his spectacles.

I commenced interpreting, however he was nervous and told the court about everything except the matter in hand. I was continually returning him to the incident and as to how it occurred.

Eventually, much to my relief, he finished.

Like it on not I thought, this is a simple case of "assault with a deadly weapon".

Crown Prosecutor Brown arose to confront the accused who was standing next to me literally shivering in his shoes.

'You have listed your occupation as that of a "nightclub photographer", is that correct Mr Douras? How often did you attend the nightclub, I mean how many nights per week?'

I interpreted and he replied, 'four nights a week.'

'Were there any side benefits from the job of photographer Mr Douras?'

As I interpreted, a puzzled expression crept over poor Constantine's face.

'What does he mean by side benefits?' he asked.

'Please Mr Brown, would you elaborate?' I requested.

'Madam interpreter, we are all over the age of 21 years, I mean was it a "pickup place" for women?' replied Brown with a sarcastic smirk. I interpreted accordingly.

'Me married, me no look for woman,' said Constantine responding in broken English.

At that stage the Judge glowered at the Prosecutor.

'Do not pursue that line of questioning sir,' he growled.

Before I could stop him, Douras poured out a torrent of Greek which confused everyone listening. As he said the following, I had no option other than to translate.

'Me stabbed her because she hit me and cut open my face,' he pointed to the angular scar below his right cheek.

'So you admit to the assault Mr Douras,' exclaimed a triumphant Stanley Brown.

'Yes me stabbed her,' cried an emotional Constantine Douras, this time in English, tears flowed down his cheeks.

I did not need to translate that, for it was in English and for all to hear.

'You can step down now Mr Douras,' crooned the Judge.

Andrew Taylor was most unhappy, he moaned removing his glasses and said rubbing his eyes. 'Oh dear, oh dear, he whispered, he has just talked himself into a nine year stretch.'

Judge Griffith — anticipating that a break in proceedings would be in order, remarked-

'Brown do you have any further questions.'

'No your Honor,' replied the Prosecutor who resumed his seat, his face wearing a smug grin.

What was the point of further questions, I thought, he's just convicted himself.

'Ladies and gentleman, the Judge said looking towards the jury, I feel it's opportune to call for a brief adjournment. I'm sure Mr Taylor will wish to have words with his client,' rasped he judge before rising, bowing and retiring to his chambers.

Andrew Taylor and I gathered around Constantine who was in tears.

'Why did he have to admit to the attack,' exclaimed my colleague.

Comforting the visibly upset Constantine, I said, 'the reason he lost control in the first place is that a woman does not strike a man on the face. In the Greek culture, it's the most degrading thing that a male can experience.'

My colleague's eyes sparkled. 'are you sure of this Mrs Gard.'

'Oh yes, I replied, that's what triggered his attack.'

'Would you enter the witness box and repeat what you have just told me?' he requested.

'Yes of course I would,' I replied.

Once again we were summoned into the Court No 4, again the Judge swept in bowing to the assembled personages. Andrew Taylor addressed his Honor.

'Your Honor I wish to call my client's interpreter to the witness box.'

The judge looked surprised. 'Why the interpreter Taylor?' he queried.

'Mrs Gard is an expert in the Greek culture your Honor, she will be able to shed a very different light on what has occurred,' replied Taylor.

This time I was returning as the prize exhibit, suddenly I realized I was in the hot seat.

Andrew Taylor commenced, 'Mrs Gard, for how long have you lived in Australia.'

'I have been in Australia for six years,' I replied. 'So you were brought up in Greece,' he observed. 'Yes, that's correct,' I responded. 'What age are you,' Taylor asked. 'I am 28 years of age,' I replied.

Taylor turned to face the jury although addressing me.

'So you lived 22 years of your life in Greece' — I agreed that was the case.

'Mrs Gard would you please repeat to the court the substance of the conversation we had a few minutes ago, he requested.

I turned in order to face both the Judge and Jury. 'In the Greek culture, the greatest insult that can be leveled at a male by a female is to strike him across the face in the manner experienced by Mr Douras.'

I looked across at the Prosecutor. Stanley Brown was sitting with a murderous gleam in his eye, for those few words had wrecked his case.

Constantine was sentenced to only eighteen months; and with good behavior he would be out in nine.

We called into his cell beneath the court to farewell him. As we shook hands, he asked in Greek. 'If I get into trouble in prison can I have your telephone number?'

Taylor turned to him saying, 'please try to behave yourself in prison and don't get into any arguments,' which I translated into Greek.

He responded with. 'What will I do if they give me a bad time in the prison - use the knife again?' A shudder ran down my spine.

'What did he say?' enquired Andrew Taylor.

'It's best you don't know,' I replied - 'let's go.'

The infamous Whisky Au Go-Go is no more - and I'm pleased to say that was the last time I have set eyes on or heard of Constantine Douras - he must be behaving himself !

Chapter 3

"Caught in the Act"

The moment he arrived I recognized him. He had dressed for the occasion — a white suit, black patent leather shoes, floral tie, black collar length hair and a gold tooth that flashed as he spoke. In short he looked a cross between "Con the Fruiter" and a former Minister of Immigration — another flamboyant dresser.

'You must be George Piperonis, I'm Angeliky Gard, your interpreter,' I said.

'Oh, I am champion weight lifter of the Mexico Olympics,' he said in Greek, shaking my hand vigorously. A client with an *attitude*, I thought to myself.

Looking at me he remarked, 'your surname is Gard?'

That it is correct, 'I'm married to an Australian', I responded.

'Oh, never mind,' he said, looking at me with a sad expression.

'What do you mean *'never mind'*, I retorted in Greek.

Sensing that I was more than a little offended, he shook his head scratching his jaw.

'It's okay, if he's a good man.' I didn't reply as many Greek's with whom I associate migrated for a better life in Australia during the early

60s. At that time — the question of language was a problem. Cultural misunderstandings were common place. Naturally families preferred their children to marry into the Greek community preserving the language, customs and culture.

Our conversation ceased abruptly when a disheveled figure, scarf streaming in the wind, ran toward us. 'Oh, I'm sorry that I am so late,' he exclaimed breathlessly. Alexander Whitehead, barrister at law, reminded me of Lewis Carroll's white rabbit, and the quote from Alice in Wonderland, 'I'm late, I'm late, for a very important date.' There he was panting, his wavy white hair flowing in the breeze and little nose glowing a bright pink.

'Oh, good, you must be Angeliky Gard,' he said recognizing me.

Turning to our client I introduced him in a mixture of the two languages.

Alexander Whitehead continued, 'our friend Mr George has been unwittingly caught up in a bank robbery.'

I was surprised, a bank robber no less.

'Perhaps you could explain what has happened Mr George?' I asked him in Greek.

Then I noticed that Mr George looked distinctly uneasy — in fact quite embarrassed.

Shrugging his shoulders he sighed deeply and looked away from me and explained.

Apparently, on occasions he would meet a girl friend in the back room of his best friend Spiro's coffee lounge in High Street Northcote. To all intents and purposes that was innocent enough if they were single, but both were married.

Mr. George was terrified his wife Roula, would find out.

His friend Manna was equally frightened her husband Manni, would learn what they had been "up to", for when provoked he was a violent man.

One evening the lovers arranged to meet in the back room of the coffee lounge, and were in the middle of — whatever lovers do on such an occasion. Suddenly there was the sound of a car racing up the service lane at the rear of the premises. Fearing the car belonged to her husband, Manna stopped whatever she was doing, gathered up her clothing running out through the front door. The patrons almost chocked their coffee. Meanwhile, George not wishing to follow and be identified as having been with Manna, ran for his life out the back door across the service lane and into the back garden of the local bank.

By pure coincidence it happened that the local Commonwealth Bank had been burgled ten minutes earlier, triggering the silent alarm, which of course summoned the police. Our client Mr George, mindful to be nowhere near his friend's coffee lounge — ran quickly into the back garden of the Commonwealth Bank to hide.

He was answering the call of nature, triggered by the severe fright he received, when the two constables arrived training their spotlights on a half naked George — literally catching him with his pants down.

Constable Valentine Plodinske (or "Plod" to his colleagues) and his partner had little to brighten their lives. Criminals had been active that week, however by the time the patrol car arrived with siren blaring, the offenders had long departed. This was the fifth call this week and their sergeant was furious. 'Listen Plod, catch them this time or I'll have you demoted to the bicycle squad. Don't think I'm joking, the matter is getting serious,' his superior growled.

Plod and partner saw this as their big chance, the Commonwealth Bank in High St Northcote had been burgled and the silent alarm triggered. This was better than a television cop show he thought – the big Falcon Pursuit sedan swung into action and they roared off siren wailing. They were not far away, actually down in Preston, for the bank was a straight run up High St. – according to the D24. message.

'On second thoughts it might be a good idea to switch off the siren, Plod said to his partner. We don't want to warn them of our arrival.' 'Okay,' he replied, switching off the siren – much to the relief of the dog population who regarded this unwelcome interruption to their slumbers, as the signal to commence choir practice.

The Commonwealth Bank hove into view, but there was no getaway car in sight.

'Oh, not again,' moaned Plod as he swung the heavy Ford around the corner and swept the rear lane with his spotlight.

Then he saw a white flash – Georges underwear. Fixing him in the spotlight, Plod shouted, 'Halt, you're under arrest.' Oh good, he thought – saved from the bicycle squad.

Our hero was not used to being caught in the middle of his ablutions, so he zipped up his trousers, looking both embarrassed and feeling threatened he fumbled with his belt.

Ah! indecent exposure as well, thought Plod, we've killed two birds with the one stone.

Grabbing their truncheons they cornered our terrified client who thought the police would punish him for his nocturnal perambulations, with Manna. 'Got you,' snarled Plod happily, 'Where's your mate?' 'Me no have mate, exclaimed Mr George, as the steel handcuffs snapped on to his wrist. 'Me no do anything wrong, me good man, why you do this?'

And so our client was transported to the Northcote Police Station where confusion reigned supreme, for Mr George spoke very little English and the police even less Greek.

Naturally at that time of night, there were no Greek interpreters to be found. Three hours of frustrating questioning followed after which Mr George was bailed by his friend, Spiro, and life at the Northcote Police Station settled back to some degree of normality. The police had given up trying to understand why he was there in the first place — so they released him.

Once, in court Plod and partner were determined to vindicate themselves in the eyes of their sergeant.

Mr George paused looking toward me for a sympathetic word. It was rather difficult as I was having a problem controlling my mirth as the episode was like something out of the "Keystone Cops", finally I recovered my composure, and looked at Mr Whitehead who was grinning like the original "Cheshire Cat."

'Well Mrs Gard, I see that you understand our friend's predicament,' observed Alexander Whitehead.

'What do we do from here,' I asked.

At that moment, a voice rang out over the court's speaker system which answered my question — "The Crown versus Piperonis."

'Here we go, said Mr Whitehead, just follow me.'

Northcote Court was a mournful structure in those days, painted in what looked like ex- Victorian Railways lavatorial green and cream paint, purchased no doubt as a Railways job lot. As we strode along the green linoleum corridor, I asked Mr Whitehead whether Manna was present?

'Yes, he said, but for obvious reasons she does not want to associate with us.'

'Actually she's over there. If you look to your right the lady in question is standing at the doorway of Court No 3, chewing gum.'

I looked across expecting a large dark lady, but no, I was wrong — she was short and slim, dressed in a low cut white top, black ski pants and shiny black open toed shoes.

'I have a sworn statement from her, but as you can understand, there is a very good reason why she doesn't want to be identified with this matter,' observed Whitehead.

Magistrate Kenneth Irons looked up as we entered court and took our seats.

'We have an attempted bank robbery and indecent exposure, is that correct ahhh — which of you is the defense barrister?'

'I am your Worship,' announced Mr. Whitehead.

'Oh, very well Mr Whitehead, and who is appearing for the Crown?' asked the magistrate peering down into the body of the Court.

The bench on which he was sitting creaked with relief as a large figure in a dark blue uniform stood to address the magistrate. 'I am your Worship, my name is Constable Valentine Plodinski, attached to the Patrol Car Division of Northcote CIB.'

' Constable Plodinski would you please proceed into the witness box', requested the magistrate.

The bulk of Constable Plod moved towards the witness box with a slow measured gait.

Taking the bible in his right hand he recited the oath without drawing breath.

Extracting a little blue notebook from his uniform pocket, he proceeded to acquaint the magistrate as to how, on the 15th day of November last, he and his partner attended a" break in" at the Commonwealth Bank in High Street, Northcote. Here much to their surprise they found our Mr George not only exposing himself but as it appeared, he was trying to leave the scene of a crime.

The Magistrate looked up from his writing, 'he was what?' he exclaimed.

'Exposing himself while trying to leave the crime scene, your Worship,' replied Plod.

'Good heavens, exposing himself and leaving the scene of the crime all at once — how extraordinary, remarked the Magistrate. I think that a reasonable person would agree, there's a time and place for everything,' he added.

There was a ripple of laughter from the body of the court — the Magistrate was starting to enjoy himself.

'Constable Plodinski, at what time did all this take place,' he asked.

Reaching for his little blue notebook Plod replied 'at 11.32 pm your Worship'

Peering down at his books the magistrate mumbled, 'your witness thank you Mr.

Whitehead.'

Alexander Whitehead strode confidently over to the witness box.

'Now I would like to ask a few questions about the events which occurred on the evening of November 15ᵗʰ last.

According to what you have told this Court, you answered a call to find my client in the grounds of the Commonwealth Bank Northcote - is that so?' — Plod nodded.

'What did you observe my client doing in the grounds of the Commonwealth Bank?' asked Alexander.

'As far as I could see the defendant was relieving himself,' replied Plod.

'So he was not engaged in running away?' said Alexander. 'No sir,' agreed Plod.

'Nothing further your Worship,' Alexander informed the magistrate.

'Mr Whitehead, would you ask your client to take the stand?' requested the magistrate.

'Certainly your Worship, we have a qualified interpreter who has been retained to assist Mr Piperonis,' advised Alexander.

Looking down at Alexander Whitehead the magistrate growled, 'how many years has your client lived in Australia?'

'I believe fifteen years your Worship,' replied Alexander.

'Well if that's the case, he should speak English,' decided the magistrate.

'Please proceed Whitehead, we haven't got all day.'

'Very well your Worship,' Alexander replied leading Mr George to the witness box.

The Clerk of Courts asked him to state his name and address and repeat after him the oath – whereupon Mr George looked at me and shrugged his shoulders.

'Mr Piperonis, would you please answer the questions and repeat the oath,' grumbled the magistrate.

George looked more puzzled than before and looked at me. 'What oath?' he asked in Greek.

The magistrate, thinking that Mr George would understand if he shouted, bellowed.

'Repeat the oath please!.' Again Mr George looked at us with a helpless expression, beads of perspiration breaking out on his forehead. Alexander Whitehead stood, 'your Worship my client does not understand English, please use the interpreter unless you want this to last all the week.'

'Oh, very well, growled the magistrate, Mrs Gard, would you step forward please.'

I entered the witness box with my client and recited the interpreter's oath.

Mr George proceeded to swear that he would answer the questions truthfully.

'Constable Plodinski, would you commence your examination,' requested the rather relieved magistrate.

'Yes your Worship, replied Plod, who again consulted his little blue book.

Mr Piperonis, would you inform the court why you were at the rear of the Commonwealth Bank in High St. Northcote on the night you were arrested?'

I turned and interpreted this in Greek to our hero who shrugged his shoulders – 'me have a pee,' he answered in Greek. When translating, I addressed the magistrate stating that my client was 'answering the call of nature, your Worship'

'Oh, I see,' said Magistrate Irons.

Constable Plod, sensing that he was losing the advantage blundered on.

'Isn't that a strange place for that purpose considering a robbery had just taken place?'

Our client paused, wiped his brow and said in Greek, 'I know nothing about any robbery, I was there because'........ then the whole sorry tale came out about his secret meetings and the fright he received when confronted by the police.

Not to be swayed, Constable Plod blundered on. 'do you honestly ask the court to believe that you entertained your friend in the back of a coffee lounge — what did you do for a bed?' To Mr. George this was the ultimate insult — for as far as he was concerned, this was tantamount to questioning his masculinity.

White with anger he yelled in English— 'if me want woman, me go to motelie!'

With that he belabored the point by striking the side of the witness box several times with his knuckles — for this man was no "cheapskate"; if he wanted to make love he was prepared to pay!

An amused titter ran through the body of the court as the magistrate glowered at Constable Plod remarked, 'was there evidence of this man's fingerprints in the bank?'

'No your Worship', replied Constable Plod.

'Well why in heavens name did you arrest him Plodinski, don't waste my court's time with this rubbish, case dismissed!' cried the magistrate, glaring at Plodinski, who no doubt wished the earth could have swallowed him whole.

So ended the case of our flamboyant lover and weight lifter George Piperonis.

The fugitive from Lewis Carroll's novel and I left Court with smiles on our faces.

I often wonder when driving through the area — if he learnt his lesson and hopefully no longer indulges in nocturnal perambulations with Mana.

I hope the latter is the case!

Chapter 4

"The Man and his Ear"

According to the Supreme Court "rumor mill" the parking supervisor Arnold Fellows, thought his territory was being invaded by a member of the "Hells Angels".

Early one morning the peace of his courtyard was shattered by the roar of a new, shiny Black Harley Davidson motor cycle as it zoomed into the Supreme Court car park.

Drawing himself up to his full 165cm, he left the comparative safety of the little courtyard office and set off to confront the interloper.

Clad in black motorcycle leathers, black helmet, visor and knee high black leather riding boots, he looked like "the creature from the black lagoon."

As Arnold Fellows approached this shiny black apparition, the subject of his approaching scorn stopped, straightened his back and removed his helmet.

'Oh hello, I do hope that it's all right for me to park my machine here?'

Before Arnold had a chance to commence his standard rebuke — ('who do you think you are, you can't park ere'), the potential subject of his scorn had removed a pass from his leathers, revealing his identity —

His Honor Judge Harold Entwhistle, of the Supreme Court of Victoria. — Arnold's demeanor changed immediately.

'Oh dear, I'm so sorry your Honor, you caught me completely by surprise. Yes certainly this position is fine. Don't worry about the question of security, I'm here until 6 pm each day. It's such a beautiful machine,' he said stroking the bike's gleaming flanks.

'Now your Honor do you know which chambers and court you have been allotted?'

'No, I'm afraid I don't,' he admitted.

'Please follow me then and I'll try to find out for you,' cooed Arnold.

Reaching inside his tiny courtyard office, removing a blue clipboard he studied it carefully for a few minutes. 'Yes, here it is, number 7, old Judge Wilson's chambers.'

Striding swiftly down the corridor leading to the chambers section of the court, Harold raised more than a few eye brows.

The man anointed as Harold's assistant was a failed legal clerk by the name of Adrian Walter, admitted him only after he produced his identification.

'Well Walter, what have we this morning?' asked Judge Harold.

'Your Honor, first on the listings is a sexual harassment case involving a severed ear.'

'Sexual harassment, and a severed ear indeed — good heavens how extraordinary.

I can't see how the two are linked,' exclaimed Judge Harold preening himself for the final time in front of the mirror.

'Now Walter, the only thing that I drink during the break is tea. Please ensure you have a supply of English Breakfast on hand, and you and I will get on fine.'

'Oh yes, your Honor', replied the subservient Walter.

The call from Mr Manier, came at 8.30 pm, the previous evening.

'We have just been given a matter in the Supreme Court, tomorrow morning. I believe it's one of sexual harassment and assault. Please ensure that you meet the barrister Mathew Parker at 9 am. by the Supreme Court's notice board.'

We lowly interpreters unfortunately do not enjoy the luxury of our own car park.

Unlike the judiciary, we must park our cars elsewhere. My favorite venue was a rabbit warren under Marland House, close to the Supreme Court, presided over by one of the most obliging parking attendants I have met, one of my countrymen, Sam — who hailed from Crete. Even when the sign outside said **CAR PARK FULL**, there was always space for me.

The Supreme Court loomed grey and black in the morning drizzle. The clever blind folded lady was still balancing the scales of justice in a rather precarious manner up there, above William Street, serving as the Hilton pigeon roost, providing accommodation for some of the thousands of birds that call Melbourne home.

Crossing a cold blustery William Street, I entered the foyer of the Supreme Court and approached the notice board. There he was, a short chubby little man wearing a tight black suit, his well oiled hair swept up and back in an 'Elvis Presley' style. He was accompanied by a thin, tall, brown haired man eagerly reading the list of cases. I approached them, speaking in English.

'Excuse me, are either of you gentlemen Mr Parker?' One of the men spun around replying — 'Yes, you must be Mrs Gard the Greek interpreter, meet Spiro Gaganaris your client.'

In duplicating the Old Bailey, our forefathers forgot the question of heating in winter, as a result the rooms and corridors are freezing. In the early 50s, some enlightened soul installed gas heating in some parts of the court complex. This concession was warmly welcomed by all, including the long suffering court staff.

Opening a frosted glass door, Matthew Parker poked his nose inside.

'Ah, this one is free, please ask your client to come inside and be seated.

Good, now let's get on with it as there are several matters which need clarifying.'

'Firstly though let's see if this jolly heater works, I'm frozen,' he said briskly rubbing his hands together.

Reaching over he pulled a cord and the ancient gas heater spluttered into life.

Turning to me he asked, 'Mrs Gard, do you know anything about this matter?'

I shook my head.

'This mild mannered little gentleman bit off his opponent's ear!'

'His what, his ear?' I sat there my mouth agape with surprise.

Facing Gaganaris, I asked him in Greek if it was true that he bit off a persons ear.

Shrugging his shoulders and extending his arms, palms outward in a very Mediterranean gesture he said 'yes'

'But why?' I asked him. He giggled in a childish manner, then looked embarrassed.

'He touched up my wife's bottom,' then the complete story unfolded.

Before I could translate, Parker interrupted us. 'Now Mrs Gard, would you please ask Mr Gaganaris to find his wife. I hope that she's here, because if not, her old man will not be around for quite a while.' I impressed upon him the importance of her presence, and a frightened Gaganaris left the room to locate her.

I filled in Parker on the details. Apparently the initial assault was perpetrated by his wife's supervisor, at her place of employment — the Mt. Olympus Dim Sim Factory.

'The – where did you say the Mt. Olympus Dim Sim Factory?' asked Parker.

'Yes, that's correct,' I replied.

'Good gracious, what ever will the Greek's get up to next? I thought the Chinese were responsible for the Dim Sim. How did the Greeks get hold of the idea?' he mused.

'Oh, I think it had something to do with Alexander the Great and his exploits in China -

he brought back the idea and the Greeks introduced it to Europe*,' I lied teasing him.

* We all know that the Greeks were responsible for invention of many things, but the Dim Sim was not among them!

Before Parker had time to reply, the wife, Vasso Gaganaris, entered the room almost blue with cold. She was an attractive lady in her early

40s, approximately 190cm in height, inappropriately dressed for the arctic conditions, in a black linen skirt, black and white check pullover, black shoes, and clutching a shiny black handbag - she looked frozen. Seizing the initiative I introduced myself and Matthew Parker, with whom she timidly shook hands.

'Ello ouw are you?' she responded.

'Mrs Gard, the question of the alleged indecent assault is extremely important to our case, as although it does not justify what happened — it gives us a better chance of getting Mr Gaganaris off with a lesser sentence. Hopefully not one that will involve him going to prison,' explained Matthew Parker.

The conference continued, with Matthew Parker firing one probing question after the other at Vasso Gaganaris, until the comparative tranquility of the room was shattered by an announcement, 'Politis V Gaganaris, Court Room Seven.'

Standing, Matthew Parker faced me, — 'right, this is where the fun begins.'

'The appointed judge is called Entwhistle — he's new. I believe a bit radical and more worldly than some of the other old duffers. He's still got his training wheels on so I think we stand the chance of a favorable hearing. Okay, we had better get going. Would you ask the clients to follow me closely; we don't want to lose them as this stage.'

Opening the door he lead us out into a corridor thronged with people, heading for Court Seven.

I followed closely with Mr & Mrs Gaganaris in my wake.

As we rounded the corner, we were confronted by a tall bearded gentleman who regarded the Gaganaris couple, with abject scorn. We had come face to face with the "opposition" in the form of Mr. J. Politis and his hairy counsel.

Shrinking back behind her husband, Vasso tried to enter the court room without provoking a reaction from Politis. Unfortunately this was not to be, for Politis snarled an insult at Vasso, "putana"(whore) which prompted me to warn him in Greek that further outbursts of this nature would only incur the wrath of the security guard.

Parker asked, 'What was that all about?' 'Oh don't worry, I told him to hold his tongue or he'd be in trouble — incidentally that's the opposition.' I replied.

Once inside the court, Mr Parker led us to the front row of seats and the two large oak tables that where provided for barristers' use. Matthew Parker lowered the bundle of files he was carrying, untying the pink ribbon holding them together, and spreading out the documents in a semblance of order. There was a movement behind us and the "opposition"

took their places. Harold Entwhistle swept into view and after bowing to all and sundry took his place on the bench. This was his first case and Justice Entwhistle looked ill at ease as he surveyed the people assembled in front of him. You could see him thinking, 'Now, which is which?'

Anticipating some judicial confusion the Grizzly Bear opposite stood, adjusting his gown. 'My name is Anthony Zagaris, I am appearing for the plaintiff.

'Would you commence please Mr Zagaris,' requested the judge.

'Your Honor, Mr Politis and Mrs Gaganaris are employed by the Mt Olympus Dim Sim Factory of Footscray, my client Politis is a bi-lingual production supervisor. Mrs Gaganaris was working on the production line packing their products. Instead of concentrating on her tasks, she has been responsible for many problems because of sick days, lateness and unproductive chatter between the women with whom she worked. She was warned on many occasions, until Mr Politis with the blessing of the management, had no option other than to dismiss her.'

While interpreting the speech to the clients I had difficulty in restraining Mrs Gaganaris, who was ready to attack Politis and his hairy barrister.

The 'Grizzly Bear' continued. 'Eventually Mrs Gaganaris was sacked; and she left most reluctantly. The following day after work, her husband lay in wait for my client attacking him. During the fight, he bit off his ear — no doubt as a form of payback.'

Harold Entwhistle turned to Michael Parker, 'I invite you to cross question the witness.'

'Your Honor, in this case our side will, while not denying liability for the assault attempt, to explain that the damage caused to Mr. Politis' ear was a direct result of his actions in respect of my client's wife'.

Parker then confirmed Politis name and occupation, one could observe Politis gaining confidence.

Suddenly Parker asked, 'are you married sir.'

'Me no married now, replied a cautious Politis.— me divorced with one child.'

Nervously glancing around, he sought the approval of his barrister who was listening.

Turning away from the plaintiff, Michael Parker continued.

'So how many people do you supervise at the Mt Olympus Dim Sim Factory?'

Thinking for a moment, Politis replied, 'about 25 ladies.'

'So you have quite a "harem" of young ladies under your control, eh?', observed Parker.

The Grizzly Bear leapt to his feet, your Honor we object to the use of the word "harem".

Judge Harold thought for a moment and uttered one word "sustained", then looking hard at Michael Parker he suggested, 'Mr Parker, kindly rephrase your last question.'

'Oh, very well your Honor,' he replied. 'Well, you certainly have a large number of ladies under your control.' Politis responded by nodding his head.

Parker continued, (so far so good), he thought.

'According to your learned counsel my client gave you problems from two angles: the first being the question of sick days, and the second punctuality. Is that correct Mr Politis?'

Politis nodded his head in agreement, his knuckles turning white as he gripped the edge of the witness box.

'Mr Politis, would you examine these time cards - 'are they from the Mt.Olympus Dim Sim Factory's office?'

Michael Parker reached across and passed Politis a handful of yellow time cards.

Politis looked worried, very, very worried. Politis agreed looking skywards he appeared to seek inspiration from the lady on the roof.

Parker continued, 'so do I have the correct picture? We have here a lonely divorced man who during the day is surrounded by 25 young ladies. You like women, don't you Mr.

Politis. Are there any problems in that respect?' he probed.

When the question of his "manhood" was at stake, Politis rose like a trout to a lure.

'Me a man, me a real man, me love women, me have balls to the ground,' he boasted.

Giggles erupted around the court at the frankness of Politis admission.

Judge Harold stopped and with pen poised, commented, 'Oh dear that could be very dangerous, eh Mr. Parker?'

I heard Parker mutter under his breath, 'He'd have to be careful not to step on them.'

Once more there was a ripple of laughter through the court.

Parker smiled, 'if that is the case, why did you recommend sacking my client, when it can be seen from the time sheets she had only been late once, and had an impeccable record in respect of sick days? Your Honor there is a lot more behind this than meets the eye. The truth is that Politis fancied his chances with Mrs Gaganaris, and when she rejected him he exacted revenge by dismissing her. This is the reason that Mr Gaganaris waylaid Politis and assaulted him. While not condoning Mr Gaganaris actions, we submit that there is irrefutable evidence of the reason for such an attack.'

The Grizzly Bear looked stunned. Judge Harold who was feeling the strain of the proceedings, having a vision of his morning tea announced, 'we'll adjourn for 15minutes.'

Bowing to all those present he swept out to his Chambers.

The rather abrupt nature of his departure took Michael Parker by surprise, for he was about to move in for the "kill".

'Okay Mrs Gard, please tell Mr and Mrs Gaganaris we will have a further discussion.'

'Mr Gaganaris, did your solicitor ask you to provide a witness as to the alleged sexual harassment?,' asked Michael Parker.

I translated the question and he nodded his head producing a grey document from his pocket. I opened the paper, and translated that Mrs Fotine Karas had witnessed the unwanted attention being bestowed on the rear end of one Vasso Gaganaris, by Mr Tassos Politis on the 14th April last, during work time at the Mt Olympus Dim Sim Factory.

I was interrupted by Mrs Gaganaris who said that there was no way the name of Karas could be used in court, on account of the lady being in fear of loosing her job.

'Don't worry about the job question, Politis will not have one after this anyway, said Parker. I'm going to call you into the witness box Mrs Gard to translate this document then we'll have him on toast.'

We returned once more to the court room — in swept Judge Harold and the case resumed.

Michael Parker addressed the judge. 'Your Honor, I call upon our interpreter to read a Statutory Declaration, which has a direct bearing on the case.' Judge Harold motioned me towards the witness box and I commenced to read it's contents. It described how Tassos Politis had been in the habit of sexually harassing Mrs Gaganaris until one night he was waylaid by her husband and beaten up. This resulted in Mrs Gaganaris' dismissal.

'Gentlemen' said Judge Harold 'it is not my intention to hear anything further on the issue of sexual harassment. I'm sure that this damming evidence does not warrant proceeding with the question of the assault. I will bear this issue in mind when I make my decision.

Mr Zagaris, would you commence.'

Zagaris sprang to his feet, 'Your Honor we wish to call John Gaganaris.'

I followed a very frightened Gaganaris into the witness box. He recited the oath and Zagaris commenced his cross examination.

'Is your name John Gaganaris, and do you live at 15 Droop St. Collingwood?'

'Yes, that is correct,' he responded in Greek. 'Are you employed or unemployed?' he asked.

I translated "unemployed."

He replied with an uncomfortable, "yes" after which he burst forth with a torrent of Greek directed at the judge. I translated it as accurately as I could until he reached – 'I had a fight with him over touching my wife's rear — he no touch my wife he would have no trouble,' he concluded in English.

Having made his point, Zagaris turned to Michael Parker saying, 'your witness.'

Parker, proceeded to reinforce the reason for the assault before sitting down to await the verdict.

Judge Harold ceased writing, and straightening his back looking directly at both Gaganaris and Politis.

'Violence cannot be condoned for any reason, let alone severing the plaintiff's ear, however I find that sexual harassment took place. The injury sustained by the plaintiff was caused by his own folly. This saved the defendant from jail. I feel however that there must be a penalty, therefore I award the sum of $2,500 to the plaintiff by way of damages.'

Upon my translation of the verdict, our client's face broke into a beaming smile.

'good, he remarked — him got money me got ear.'

Michael Parker muttered to me, 'I hope he enjoyed it.'

Judge Harold's first day on the Bench had been a frustrating experience.

The silk robes were uncomfortable, the wig irritated both his face and neck.

He gratefully disrobed, changing into his black Planet Hollywood shirt and jeans, then pulled on his Reebok boots. Reaching for his diary, he looked in his brief case for a highlighter to mark a page in his diary.

'Oh darn it, he muttered, I've left it in my desk on the bench.'

He opened the door of his chambers leading to the court room, to be confronted with a sea of faces, mouths agape.

It had been a difficult first day indeed for His Honor Justice Harold Entwistle, Judge of the Supreme Court of Victoria and biker, — his associate, surprised by the abrupt nature of Judge Harold's exit, had yet to dismiss the court.

Chapter 5

"The Man and the
Insurance Company Affair"

The reader may or may not be aware of the change in the law dealing with personal injury and workers compensation claims. It was a vain attempt to stem the tide of the enormous strain on insurance companies coffers and demands on the courts' time. Previously, if an insurance company decided to go to court regarding a disputed claim, the action was funded initially by the company. Now the onus of funding the action has to be borne by the claimant.

Most of my cases in this area have been settled prior to the matter finding its way to court, however sometimes settlements take place in the corridors just before the case starts.

Insurance companies tend to haggle and adopt these tactics when they consider the claim excessive in an endeavor to avoid a large payout.

The question of the claim's legitimacy is of course the burning question. In order to ensure their own viability, indeed survival, insurance companies employ investigators to spy on applicants in an attempt to disprove the legitimacy of their claim in court. These days the odds are stacked in the insurance companies favor, resulting in the aggrieved having to think twice before proceeding — given the huge financial commitment involved in funding a case.

The level of workers compensation fraud has spawned a whole new industry, namely an occupation particularly popular with disaffected or retired members of the police force.

In many cases the investigators have saved the insurance industry many millions of dollars, however in other cases they have made serious errors.

This following is a story about one of them!

The original Workers Compensation Board, scene of verbal jousting, tears and a few miracles (see Chapter 10) was housed on the 22nd floor of an enormous city building towering into the sky at 570 Bourke Street Melbourne.

Here, compensation for work related injuries have been haggled over and debated, outcomes agreed upon and financial compensation awarded to soothe the aggrieved and their injuries.

Owen Dixon Chambers are busy at the best of times, however close to 4pm, cases are concluding, clerks run to and fro pushing trolleys bulging with files.

To add to the confusion, barristers clad in their black legal regalia complete with white horsehair wigs, scurry about, trying hard not to collide with each other.

On one such afternoon I joined a group of people, waiting at the lift door, trying to reach the floor of their choice in the shortest possible time. I noticed a dark middle aged gentleman, obviously injured and in some pain waiting in the crowd to join the group of prospective passengers. As we entered, the lift doors closed with a soft thud and we ascended to the 5th level. They softly hissed open and I stepped outside followed by the injured gentleman.

I was seeking Room 512, the legal chambers of John Buxton - Barrister at Law.

A grey haired, bearded, bewigged and gowned John Buxton looked up from his desk as we entered. Then I realized that my fellow traveler must be my client — Panos' Asimakis.

When we were seated, Buxton asked me to translate Panos' story.

We commenced with details of the accident: 'I worked for a Company called Parkview Constructions for a period of eight years, during which I assisted in constructing many of the tall buildings in the Melbourne central business district. On 25th of May I was working as a laborer, pushing a large wheelbarrow full of wet concrete when I slipped and fell, injuring my back. I was taken to hospital, they treated me for a week, afterwards I was able to return to my home, with instructions to rest.

Since then, I have seen doctor after doctor who all agree I am not going to improve, and I am entitled to a pension or a lump sum payment.'

Buxton nodded sympathetically. 'Yes, as I can see the reports back this up, and in spite of that, the stupid people at Newhaven still want this to go before the Board.'

'Now my man,' he said looking straight at us. 'Please Mrs Gard this is important, I want his assurance that he has not been doing any work - regardless.'

Panos looked at me in surprise when I translated what had been said.

'Mrs Angeliky, he said in Greek with tears welling in his eyes — please tell this man that I am not capable of doing anything.'

'Okay Mr. Panos, I replied trying to placate him, the barrister has to be sure, that's the reason he asked you again.'

'Please excuse me a moment,' Buxton said reaching for the telephone. I'm phoning the barrister appearing for the Newhaven Insurance mob, and we'll see if we can short circuit the whole business, without going before the Board.'

'Joe Brixton please,' he rasped into the telephone.

'Joe, good afternoon this is John Buxton. I have a Mr Asimakis, I believe you have the relevant correspondence on this case from Michael Morgan the instructing solicitor.

Yes - that's the one, you know the details of the matter. Okay Joe, what about us — he broke off in mid sentence. Oh, I see, okay you say there is no room to maneuver. Okay Joe, if you say so however knowing the facts of the case I feel ….' he stopped again.

'Right,' he snarled if that's how you're thinking - okay!'

His face was a flushed red as he slammed the phone down on its cradle.

He says they'll fight and they have conclusive evidence — if that's what they want, all right we'll fight,' he said thumping the desk in exasperation.

'Mrs Gard would you be kind enough to inform our friend that as scheduled we will take on the Newhaven Insurance Company tomorrow 10am sharp, at Workers Compensation Board.' With that he closed the conference and we departed, descending once more to the organized mayhem that was Owen Dixon Chambers.

The following day Buxton was to be joined by Michael Morgan the instructing solicitor.

Buxton looked at me saying, 'now Mrs Gard, we have to ask our client once more, has he undertaken any work either full or part time? I know that he will not take very kindly to this but my query is not without a reason.'

Anticipating that the question would not be well received by my client, I tried to ask him as diplomatically as I could.

'Mrs Angela, Panos replied in Greek - I have already told this man on a number of occasions that I am unable to do any work, that is the position - he does not seem to want to accept it.'

'It's okay', I replied, I will tell him once more, but please remember he's only trying to help you.'

Nodding his head, 'yes, I understand,' he responded.

Addressing my colleagues, I assured them. 'The answer is the same gentlemen, he is absolutely emphatic that he has not, and what's more cannot undertake anything relating to employment because of the condition his back is in.'

John Buxton tugged his beard thoughtfully nodding. 'Okay, we won't approach that question again, as I don't want to upset him prior to having his day in the witness box.'

The atmosphere in the Workers Compensation Board is more informal than a court.

The board rooms are similar, however cases are heard by a panel of three judges who, unlike the County and Supreme Courts, are neither robed or wigged, conducting proceedings in suits and ties. The result is that it is far less intimidating.

The opposition arrived occupying the right hand side of the bench which stretched from one side of the room to the other - we sat on the left side.

A door opened and the three judges entered, placing their files on the bench in front of them before bowing to both parties, who returned their gesture.

The centre judge spoke. 'Good morning gentlemen and, I believe, madam interpreter.

I understand that we have a claim for personal injury in front of us.

It has been brought by a Panos Asimakis against the Newhaven Insurance Company,' he said staring down into the body of the room.

Both barristers nodded in unison.

'We understand the claimant has been severely injured while working as a laborer for Parkview Constructions.'

'That's correct your Honor, responded Buxton. A prolonged period of ongoing medical attention has been received by my client as evidenced in the medical reports,' he said lifting a bulging file. A green uniformed usher moved forward and Buxton handed them over, to be placed in front of the centre judge who looked surprised by the sheer volume.

'Gentlemen, as you can no doubt understand, there is quite a deal of reading involved.

It is our intention to call an adjournment of say 45 minutes during which we will have time to read the reports and jointly assess and discuss the contents.'

The tension eased somewhat and John Buxton turned to us saying, 'Angela please take our friend out into the foyer — buy him a cup of coffee or something, but don't let him out of your sight. Michael and I are going to try and "talk turkey" with our friends the opposition.'

With that and before I had a chance to explain to Panos what had transpired, they departed. Later, I observed Buxton and Brixton were involved in animated discussion.

Suddenly our barrister became agitated, slapping his fist on the pile of documents he was carrying, before returning red faced and visibly upset.

'That Brixton, he exclaimed is aptly named — as tough as a brick and twice as thick.

Now where's that coffee?' he declared reaching into his pocket for a coin.

'I take it you have had no success negotiating,' I ventured.

'Absolutely none,' he responded. 'I cannot understand it.

'The reason I'm concerned is they vow and declare that they are in possession of enough evidence to suggest our friend is a fraud.'

Finishing the last of our coffee, we returned to Room 4 and resumed our seats.

A door creaked open on the left hand rear wall of the room, and the judges filed in looking for all the world like the "three wise men". Brixton leaped to his feet, no doubt fearing the judges response after reading the medical reports.

'Your Honor's, rather than waste the Board's time with cross examination, could I suggest that we adjourn to the viewing room.

We can substantiate the reason that the claim has been denied by the insurance company.'

The judges were somewhat taken aback by the outburst.

The centre judge remarked, 'do you mean that you wish to forgo your right to cross examine the claimant?' 'Yes your Honor', Brixton replied.

The three judges proceeded to discuss his request in hushed tones. Eventually the centre judge declared - 'Oh very well, this matter is adjourned to the viewing room on the 21st Floor.'

I looked at John Buxton who was as white as a sheet. 'This is the last thing I expected Angela, they've obviously had this "up their sleeve" all the time,' he exclaimed.

'Usher please turn off the lights and lets get on with it,' one of the judges commanded.

Upon extinguishing the lights the darkness was absolute. The only glimmer of light came from the interior of the projector. Then the machine flicked into life, the opening scene showed a man of Panos appearance carrying what appeared to be a box of apples. The location changed to the front of a house in what appeared to be the Northcote area.

Before the camera could zoom in for a close up, Panos had jumped to his feet.

Waving his arms in the air shouting in broken English and Greek. 'That's not me Mrs Angela, please tell them that's my twin brother Fanos.'

'What did he say Angela,' asked John Buxton, his voice eager with anticipation. I laughed aloud, 'Buxton and his "Merry Men" have been spying on the wrong man.

This is Fanos - Panos's twin brother.'

This was the day that the Insurance Company and its investigators made the classic error of spying on the wrong person — very difficult when there were "twins" involved.

So ended the matter of "Panos and "Fanos" — I'm pleased to say that the Court settlement he received enabled him to enter into a comfortable retirement.

Chapter 6

"The Ladies and the Shoplifting Caper"

My phone rang. 'Hi Angela, this is Anthoula, I was wondering whether you can help me as I'm stuck in the Supreme Court on a case which I think will never finish.!'

Anthoula, was born on one of the most beautiful Greek islands - Lefkas, a slice of heaven in the west, below the island of Corfu. Originally a member of the Interpreter's Club, but now instead of freelancing, she chose to set up her own interpreting agency. It had been a long haul for her, so friends you can rely on are important. I am privileged to be counted as one.

'Actually I have one appointment to attend, however I'll drive over and deal with your clients as soon as I can,' I reassured her Ferntree Gully is a working class suburb of outer Melbourne some 30 kilometers from the city centre, at the foot of the Dandenong Ranges. Melbourne's suburban sprawl has spread to where there were once waving orchards of fruit tree blossom as far as the eye could see. Now, new suburbs have sprung up rather like the carpets of mushrooms which used to shelter under the trees. Development in the area has been unkind. Light industry had introduced a harder edge, effectively destroying the tranquil country atmosphere previously enjoyed by Ferntree Gully and the lower reaches of the "Dandenongs".

Fortunately, development has not extended into the hills of the Dandenong Ranges, so this beautiful mountainous Eden remains largely undisturbed. It's a region which reminds me of the waterfall town of Edessa set on a plateau high above the Plains of Macedonia in Northern Greece.

The Dandenong Ranges was the home of the "bell" birds. Seldom seen, their calls fill the air with the sound of thousands of tinkling crystal bells. Then there are the lyrebirds, and the clouds of multi colored parrots which screech a greeting.

In the 1930s, Ferntree Gully was a hiker's delight. In those days the electric train line ended there, and a beautiful little steam train called "Puffing Billy" took over, serving the tiny settlements of Upwey, Tecoma, Belgrave and Emerald, nestled in the vast forests which cloak the mountains. In those days, bed and breakfast establishments and tea shops flourished, ensuring a continual flow of people year round from Melbourne and interstate.

Sadly times change. These days the electric train travels through Ferntree Gully up into the Dandenong Ranges. A concession to nostalgia however has been the retention of the now famous "Puffing Billy" a steam engine, operating on weekends and holidays, no doubt staffed by some of the youngsters it carried who have grown up yearning for the past.

Police station's never are inspiring places and Ferntree Gully's was no exception.

Most confronting are the number of notices adorning the walls describing characters sought by the police. A tall policeman confronted me at the counter — from his appearance he gave the impression of being an escapee from "Bluey Day". He was completely bald, the top of his head reflecting the yellowish glow of an ancient flickering fluorescent light.

'Thank goodness you're here' said Constable Rossiter after I had introduced myself.

We have a couple of Greek shoplifters in the interview room. we can't make head nor tail of them, or they of us.'

Opening a small door in the counter I followed him to the rear, where he entered a small featureless room ushering me inside.

'And about time too,' I was greeted in Greek by two of the most irate ladies I had ever met. One shouted at me angrily in Greek, 'do you know how long these idiots have kept us. It's like being in prison and I have my husband's dinner to prepare!'

'Oh dear, I don't to deserve this," I thought; turning to them I replied in Greek.

'I am an independent interpreter, and you two have caused me a great deal of inconvenience - having to come all the way out here.

This is a long way from where I live, count yourselves lucky that I' m here at all, and you're not locked up for the night! Then what would you be saying to your husbands?'

My outburst stopped them completely in their tracks, they stared in disbelief. Senior Constable Rossiter also was taken by surprise — he stood back and waited for the dust to settle.

'What's wrong with them Mrs Gard?' he asked with a puzzled expression.

'Oh don't worry about them, I replied. They're rather upset about being kept waiting, but I've explained the position they're in.'

'Did you really — good for you,' remarked Senior Rossiter, concealing a wry smile.

'Okay, please tell me their story,' I requested -after drawing up a chair and sitting down.

Senior Rossiter slipped into policeman mode. 'It has been alleged by two K-Mart store detectives that the two ladies were observed helping themselves to stock in ladies underwear before attempting to leave without paying. When approached they were asked if they were in possession of stolen goods. This question was not replied to, owing to the language problem, which has resulted in their detention.'

When he paused for breath I turned to the ladies trying another angle.

'The police maintain you have been caught shoplifting — what do you say to that?'

There was no response, so I proceeded. 'I need to know your names if I am going to help you sort out this matter.'

The eldest reached into the black leather bag she was carrying. 'My name is Mrs.

Phoeffe Costas, High School Certificate Graduate from Larissa in 1958 - see I have my Certificate, look here,' she said thrusting a worn document into my hand.

This is not the Greek way to introduce yourself - showing your High School Certificate, but pride had got the better of her — she had been educated and wanted us to know it!

'Now look Mrs.Costas, this has absolutely nothing to do with your charge,' I responded.

The security staff found you and your friend stealing articles from the K-Mart store in East Burwood. What's the name of your friend?' I asked.

She huffed and puffed, 'Her name is Helen Kafos'

Her friend sat quietly, without contributing to the conversation. I was in no mood to be trifled with. 'How do you explain the two sets of underwear found in your possession?'

I asked.

Phoeffe Costas shrugged her shoulders, and spread her hands expressively, 'I don't know, maybe they just fell into my bag,' she suggested.

'If you're ready Mrs Gard, I would like to prepare their statement,' said Senior Rossiter.

He began typing a legal document with one finger using an ancient Remington typewriter, halting occasionally to ask questions.

I faced Mrs Costas asking her bluntly in Greek — 'why did you steal these articles?'

Mrs. Costas looked embarrassed.

'It was the devil who made me do it,' she confessed to me.

I interpreted this to Senior Rossiter, who was struggling not to laugh. The two proud women were a hopeless pair of criminals. The document was finally complete. Senior Constable Rossiter handed me the statement and I turned to them, saying in Greek, 'ladies you are charged with shoplifting. I will translate this statement and after signing it you are free to go.'

They grudgingly agreed that the contents were correct, and signed their names.

'The police cannot do this to me, I'm a High School Graduate,' complained Phoeffe 'Please be quiet, go home and find yourself a solicitor because you'll need one' I replied curtly for they had tested my patience enough.

I thought that was the last I would see of our hopeless pair of shoplifters — not so!

About a month later I accepted an appointment before realizing who was involved.

So on a sunny Monday morning I arrived at the Ferntree Gully Courthouse to fulfill an interpreting appointment. I had no problem recognizing my clients. They were talking in an animated manner with a short balding bearded gentleman who was battling to understand.

When I approached, he had his back toward me - the clients pretended I was not there, treating me as the enemy. I decided I had been ignored for long enough, so I introduced myself.

I recognized the man as Izzey Lotman, a barrister whose rooms I had visited once before in Preston.

'I have read the charges, and it appears to be very much an open and shut case of shoplifting. They have signed the copies acknowledging their misdemeanor.

It only remains for me to try to convince the magistrate this was a "one off" mistake.'

'Okay, I'll leave it to you', I said.

Moving over to the two clients who were still trying to ignore me, I spoke to them.

Apparently they were fearful their names would appear in the Greek Newspapers, bringing shame on their families. Their fear prompted a truce. 'Mrs Angela, what do you think will happen?' they asked.

'I honestly have no idea, this whole matter will be decided by the Magistrate,' I replied, not daring to venture an opinion. I had no desire to be on the receiving end of their wrath if the decision was worse than I anticipated.

Our conversation ceased abruptly when their case was announced. We moved into the Court, a small room with cream walls containing heavy stained 'turn of the century' furniture.

His Worship, John Lothian was literally up to his elbows in files, as he struggled to keep abreast of developments that morning. The work flow had been constant. The number of drug cases had delayed him, so he was forced to work through his morning break in order to clear the backlog of cases — hopefully before lunch.

I noticed Sergeant Rossiter seated with another uniformed member. He beckoned to me.

'Angela, meet Bill Greenwood who is prosecuting.'

Nodding to Sergeant Rossiter and Izzey Lothman the magistrate enquired, 'which case are you two gentlemen and lady involved in?'

His clerk, a bespectacled spotty young man arose placing the relative file on the overladen Magistrate's desk. Sergeant Greenwood stood to commence the case by delivering his version of the events contained in the record of interview, which noted the ladies confessions.

'Can I have both of the accused in the witness box please Mr Lothman, the interpreter can stand outside,' suggested the magistrate.

When I explained the magistrates request the ladies followed me, pale and shaking.

'Please madam interpreter swear in the accused,' requested the Clerk of Courts.

Frightened, the ladies took the oath in a whisper, heads bowed staring at the floor in shame.

'Now, madam interpreter, it is most important that you make these two ladies aware of exactly what I have to say, remarked the magistrate looking stern. Ladies, the law regards shoplifting as a punishable crime, shoplifting costs retailers hundreds of thousands of dollars each year. Society demands that apprehended shoplifters are treated harshly. In this case you have both confessed, therefore I will take this into account, along with the fact that this is your first conviction and hopefully last.'

Magistrate John Lothian focused on Izzey Lothman.

'Sir, do you have anything further to add to the contents of this record of interview'?

'Your honor our, my clients have asked me to speak on their behalf. At the time of the incident they had both been in Australia for ten years. During that time they have not had as much as a parking conviction against their names. This incident has caused a great deal of embarrassment to them and their families.

They are sincerely sorry for what has occurred — it was a momentary lapse which will never be repeated.'

The Magistrate paused, 'would the accused and their interpreter please stand.

It is my finding that as the accused admit to participating in the crime of shoplifting, I am placing you both on a twelve month's good behavior bond of $1000 each. In addition you are to donate $200 each to the court's "Poor Box". Ladies, I do not want to see your faces ever again in my court.'

When the Magistrate's finding was translated, they burst into tears, promising in Greek they would never steal again, repeating how much they regretted what had occurred.

I believed them — their pride had taken such a severe battering I doubt that they would ever be guilty of so much as a Parking Infringement or an overdue library book.

Chapter 7

"The Man and his Proxy"

The weekends are sacred in our household. During the week I am on call, on a 24 hour basis, and must be available if a Greek interpreter is required. - I reluctantly accepted a request to attend the Prahran Police Station early one Saturday evening.

'We have a rather strange situation here. It would appear there are people at the station alleging that an abduction has taken place. I wonder if it is possible for you to help us?'

I had no option other than to agree to attend.

Upon my arrival I walked into a scene of utter pandemonium, with at last 20 people of Mediterranean origin gathered at the front counter facing a solitary policeman who was vainly trying to calm them.

Excusing myself, I had to push my way to the front and tried to introduce myself.

'Are you Angeliky Gard, the Greek interpreter?' shouted the beleaguered policeman.

'Yes I am,' I shouted back over the commotion.

'Thank goodness for that, he replied. We are in all sorts of trouble with these people.'

He opened a side door and I was ushered inside. Facing the throng of people, I raised my hands clapping loudly. At the sound of the loud "bangs", the commotion ceased abruptly.

I addressed them in Greek. 'Ladies and gentlemen, could I have your attention please? I am the police interpreter. Obviously I cannot talk to all of you at once, can I speak to one of you at a time please.'

A tall, muscular man, pushed his way to the front of the crowd.

'Mrs Angeliky, my name is Adonis Papadopoulos, I can explain what has happened.'

Then the story started to unfold.

The birthplace of Nicholas, the principal character in the story, was Edessa - a sleepy little town some 700 kilometers from Athens. Set high on a mountain plateau above the Plains of Macedonia, it froze in winter and baked in summer. The great plane trees cloaking the entire plateau, were watered by eight huge cataracts which thundered through the town, providing not only a cool respite in the summer, but hydro electricity to the surrounding countryside the year round.

It was here in days of old that King Philip of Macedon, and his court sought refuge from the searing heat of the Athenian summers.

Many townsfolk chose to leave Edessa's leafy glades and emigrate to cities such as Melbourne and Sydney, Australia, in the late 1960s searching for a better life. The Boukos family however, decided to stay and concentrate on making at best a meager living from growing grapes and raising sheep. They raised their son Nicholas in this tranquil rural environment, the harsh winter melting to a mild spring, the searing summers cooling to golden Hellenic autumns.

Since a small boy however, Nicholas continued to hear of the good life his relatives were enjoying living in Australia. His elder brother Steven had settled in Sydney, marrying one of the village girls. At 28 years of age, Nicholas's parents were starting to worry.

Nicholas tried to find a bride — but there were few young girls of marriageable age left in the area. Then it happened — his brother's friend Adonis, living in Sydney, wrote to him suggesting that it was about time he married. Adonis had heard of a beautiful young girl called Persofoni who was willing to meet him. The enclosed photograph set his pulse racing.

Would he come to Australia on the basis of a proxy marriage?

Nicholas was immediately impressed.

A passport and visa were arranged, and before he knew it, he was boarding a huge QANTAS 707.V. Jet, bound for Australia.

The journey almost killed him, why was Australia so far?

Some 36 hours after leaving Athens he was preparing to land in Sydney.

Steven and his new wife were at Sydney Airport to meet him; they embraced and talked as they collected Nicholas's luggage for transfer to the domestic terminal where he would board a smaller aircraft for the journey to Melbourne. 'I'm sure you will be as happy as I am,' Steven assured Nicholas as he commenced boarding.

An hour later, the Boeing 727 jet, touched down at Melbourne's Essendon Airport.

Initially he was unsure as to who would meet him, but then he heard a Greek voice calling him, 'Nicholas Boukos!' he faced a group of people, bearing bunches of flowers.

'Are you the relatives of Persephoni,' he asked extending his hand, which was seized and shaken vigorously by all. 'Welcome Nicholas, welcome,' they cried.

'Where is she?' he exclaimed.

'Oh don't you worry for you'll meet her soon enough,' they assured him.

Melbourne was so different to Greece, everything seemed flat. However the roads well made and so wide. There were flowers and well manicured green lawns in front of the houses. North West Melbourne soon became Richmond, and then Windsor, as the big Valiant Charger roared towards his home and the first meeting with the beautiful Persephoni.

Down a tree lined street, swept the Charger, stopping outside an old double fronted Victorian house painted sky blue and white. Out he jumped, the front door opened and she stepped out into the garden - the woman of his dreams. The Aphrodite of modern day Windsor, ran out into the sunlight towards him, her arms outstretched. He wanted to cry out in anger.

This was not the woman depicted in the photograph. Here stood a lady almost half as old again as he. She was short, blonde, and fat. 'Oh no,' he thought, there has been a terrible mistake w He quickly realized he was trapped, the only way out for him was to run away but not immediately. He had done nothing wrong, however his brother was far away in Sydney — how would he get there? 'Welcome to Australia,' said Persephoni warmly embracing him.

The relatives stood back, nodding their heads and smiling, 'Yes,' he could hear them thinking.

'this is a match made in heaven.' 'Heaven's going to be unlucky this time' he resolved.

After a huge meal lovingly served by Persephoni, he excused himself as being tired, went to the room they had prepared for him and closed the door.

At this stage I raised my hand, 'was it the next day that he disappeared,' I asked.

'Yes,' replied Adonis. 'Okay you did say at one stage that he had a brother in Sydney?' I asked.

'Yes,' he replied. 'Do you have a telephone number?' I asked.

'No,' he replied, but I have his address as 12, Railway Terrace Randwick.'

'Leave this to me, go home. I'll call you as soon as I have some answers.' I responded.

After some searching, I managed to find Steven Boukas' telephone number.

The story resumes back in Melbourne — Nicholas opened his wallet; where was the telephone number given to him in Sydney by Steven - finally he found it.

When his hosts (and Persephoni) departed for work the next day he planned his escape.

Telephoning John Pappas the taxi driver known to his brother, he explained his predicament. He didn't even know the address of where he was staying.

'Please John, help me,' he implored. 'Okay, said John, I will telephone Steven in Sydney and find his address.

Call again in 15 minutes and I'll arrange your escape.'

After what seemed an eternity, Nicholas telephoned John once more.

'Okay I know where you are,' said John, meet me just past the house at 2 am, I drive a yellow taxi.'

That night, Nicholas collected only the bare minimum of his possessions, leaving most of his clothes in their suitcases. He made good his escape by climbing quietly out the bedroom window and disappearing into the night.

Punctually at 2am, John Pappas taxi swept into the street — Nicholas introduced himself and stowed his possessions in the boot before entering the taxi.

'Please take me to my brother, he cried in terror, I must escape because if they find me I'm in big trouble. I'm very afraid.'

John Pappas did not need any further prompting. Off they went, the taxi heading through the city and out on Sydney Rd bound for Sydney.

Some 12 hours later the taxi drew up outside Steven's home, 1200 kilometers away from Persephoni and her family.

Steven and his wife Maria were shocked.

'What on earth are you going to do?' they asked.

John Pappas, the good friend, suggested they wait until the family in Melbourne settled down. Meanwhile, not one to pass up a golden opportunity, he hatched a plot of his own. Two days later, his sister Roula, a buxom little lady in her late 20's came up by train from Melbourne. She was introduced to Nicholas — the chemistry was right, and they became engaged. The happy couple rode back to Melbourne in the rear of John's taxi.

To all intents and purposes that was the end of the story, however it was my duty to contact Adonis and his family to explain that an abduction had not taken place and to gently tell him - 'the bird had flown.'

He and his family were in shock. I discussed the matter with the police and they agreed to close the book on the matter.

The last news of them was they had produced two huge sons, both of whom graduated from Melbourne's Latrobe University with Bachelor of Arts Degrees. One became a teacher, and the other an architect.

Postscript.

Some years later, whilst interpreting another case, I learnt of another chapter in the saga.

Apparently when young ladies from Edessa, including Anna for whom I was acting, first came to live in Melbourne, John Pappas and his wife took it upon themselves, out of the kindness of their hearts, to provide food and shelter. Eventually jobs and a place to live were found. Anna remembered Nicholas and Roula's marriage. Two days before the actual wedding, without warning, the girls were told to move out to temporary accommodation.

No reason was given, they just had to comply with Johns request.

John Pappas was not silly, he didn't want Nicholas to change his mind for the second time!

Chapter 8

"The Dictator of Carringbush"

Grace called me early one Monday morning in the middle of our winter.

'Angeliky, is it possible for you to attend the Carringbush Town Hall?'

Apparently there is a hall next door in which the local Greek Elderly Citizens Club meet; they are in need of an interpreter.'

I thought to myself that's strange, they're Greeks and they need an interpreter?

'Okay Grace, I responded, what time do they want me to arrive?'

'As soon as you can please Angeliky, there seems to be some sort of ongoing problem,' she replied giving nothing away.

Down the Eastern Freeway I drove, then off in the direction of Carringbush.

The Town Hall looked more depressingly greyer than usual, as I arrived and parked my car. Moving through the front door, I noticed a number of elderly men and one woman gathered around a large conference table. The woman swung around addressing me in English when she realized who I was.

'Oh thank heaven you've arrived - the language question is getting the better of us.

We are having such a problem understanding each other.'

I'm Julie Harris from Carringbush Council, here at the request of the Secretary of the Greek Elderly Citizens Club. There appears to be a problem with the president who cannot understand the limit of his power under their constitution.'

'Which one of you is the President?' I asked in Greek.

'Me President,' replied a short, round little man with a shiny bald pate, who looked at me with a fierce expression as he arose to shake my hand. Oh dear here's trouble, I thought.

'I am the Secretary,' said a tall dark bespectacled gentleman in Greek.

The President approached me appearing to be annoyed at the fact there were two outsiders invading his domain!

'Why are you here - you not old enough to join our club,' he declared glaring at me.

Thankfully I agreed with him!

'Let's get one thing straight from the start, I responded, I am not here to join your club, but at the request of the Carringbush Council. You obviously have a problem that Julie and I are going to try to help you solve.'

I looked firmly at the President - somewhat taken aback, he replied in Greek -.

'I am the President — this man, pointing to the secretary he shouted — he do what I say.'

I translated this to Julie, who had retreated to the sidelines following his outburst.

'Well no Angeliky, this is not quite correct,' she replied - please inform the gentleman that according to the constitution he can act as president and do nothing else apart from the supervision and delegation of various committee members tasks. The President for instance does not deal with the day to day matters involved in the operation of the club. That is left to the individual members of the Committee.'

Julie stopped and waited for me to translate this into Greek.

The result was immediate. The President shook his fist at the Secretary in a most threatening manner shouting - 'I kill you, you b.....d,' in Greek, glaring at him fiercely.

The atmosphere became explosive.

The Secretary responded. Unwilling to be shouted down by this man, obviously ignorant of the constitutional rules and unwilling to listen to Julie's explanation.

'If you're a man come outside and we'll settle this,' he said removing his coat and rolling up his sleeves.

Blue in the face the President obliged, taking off his coat, rolling up his sleeves and to our surprise and horror, prepared by removing his false teeth placing them on the table.

'Goodness, I agreed to come here I didn't anticipate they'd start attacking each other.

please Angeliky we can't let this situation continue, tell them to calm down or I'll call the police. Really these gentlemen should know better' – Julie admonished them 'Now Mr President, please restore your false teeth to their rightful place, roll down your sleeves. There will be no more fighting over this matter,' I instructed firmly.

'Butttt Mrs.Angela,' the President commenced in Greek.

'That is the law,' I stated firmly — determined not to put up with any nonsense.

Seizing the opportunity I said, 'Okay Julie, I think that the position is clear, they understand the terms under which they have to operate, so if you are agreeable I think it's time to depart.'

'Goodbye gentlemen,' I said in Greek — we both have other appointments, so if there is nothing further we will leave.'

They assured us that they understood the position, and would operate accordingly.

The Secretary arose and shook hands, thanking us profusely in Greek, as we moved towards the front door.

'On behalf of the club, I can only say how much we appreciate the time you have taken to advise us on this problem. I can assure you that the President understands his position. We are all most grateful for your presence.'

We said our "goodbyes" and made good our escape.

While I was discussing the matter with Julie outside we heard thumps and the screaming of some colorful Greek words speculating on the supposed parentage of one of the protagonists.

'Oh Angeliky, what are they saying?' asked an anxious Julie.

'It's better that you don't know,' I replied entering my car — let's go, remember they have an election coming up shortly, so hopefully that will sort out matters once and for all.'

Prior to reaching my next appointment, I received a message to return, as the Carringbush police found two elderly gentlemen fighting in the street outside the Town Hall.

'Oh no', I thought — that has a very familiar ring about it.

As soon as practicable I returned to the scene of the morning fracas. Sure enough it was the same two protagonists. The police were amused when they discovered the reason for the "fist-a-cuffs", deciding it would be preferable for me to dress them down on their behalf.

I entered the interview room to find two of the most contrite characters I had ever seen.

'You two should be ashamed, men of your age fighting in the street like a couple of "Vlachos"(hillbilly's) — what will your families, let alone the Greek community think of you.

Both of you are a disgrace. Do you realize if this gets out, the club will lose its meeting place,'

I threatened them.

'After I spoke to the police, they have agreed not to put you both on a charge —

however in the event of a repeat of your performance, you will find yourselves in jail.'

'Do I make myself clear?'

The President raised his head to speak — I held up my hand and stopped him.

'You are both free to go, but remember I do not want to see you ever again.'

Postscript - Well, the day was not such a disaster — on my way home, there he was, one of our ex Premier's famous for his "big mouth" sitting quietly in his grey/blue BMW stuck in Punt Road traffic trying to look inconspicuous.

Deciding not to inflate his ego any further, I chose to observe what was happening out of the corner of my left eye. He was caught in the traffic like a cork in a bottle, unable to go left or right, backwards or forwards, glancing around furtively while he sat willing the lights to change.

Two small boy's traveling in the rear the car in front were making their political loyalties very obvious - by way of some expressive one fingered digital gestures.

I couldn't help but feel sorry for him!

Chapter 9

"The Man and his travels"

Architecture has never held much fascination for me, except perhaps just a sneaking admiration for the art deco magnificence of the "Cornhill Towers" building at the professional end of St Kilda Rd. close to St Kilda junction. I have occasionally teased its tenants- mainly medical professionals, that one of these days the developers will get hold of the building, and its art deco magnificence will be lost for ever.

Today my travels took me to this building. My appointment was scheduled at the rooms of Dr John Smedley, regarded by his associates as the "Marco Polo" of the medical profession - my client was a lady called Katina Kariss.

Entering the foyer I found a large plaque attached to one of the lime green stucco walls informing all and sundry that the "Cornhill Towers" building had been officially classified by the National Trust — my joking prediction would never become a reality.

Pausing, I smiled to myself, both surprised and delighted — this beautiful building had been saved from the wrecker's hammer. Such foresight would ensure that it will remain for future "Melburnians" to enjoy.

I pressed the button and woke from my dreaming when the ancient lift arrived with a "bang" and the door opened. The antique conveyance jerked angrily into life and wheezed up to the third floor where it stopped with a jerk, that almost knocked me over. The door opened with a resounding crash and I ventured into the corridor towards the frosted glass door which announced the "rooms" of Dr John Smedley M.D.

The smiling face of Dr Smedleys receptionist Delia greeted me. 'Hi Angela, how are you? I noticed that you had an appointment with doctor to interpret for Mrs Kariss.

I'm so pleased to see you again, it's been a while.'

Delia was indeed part of the furniture, diplomatic, trustworthy and above all utterly loyal — as many envious employers discovered when they tried to lure her away.

'I notice that you (the building I mean) had been listed by the National Trust.

How do you feel about that? I bet you're pleased,' I remarked.

'Absolutely delighted,' she replied.

At that moment there was another shattering crash, as the lift disgorged another passenger who limped into the waiting room.

The lady looked Greek, so taking the advantage I asked in Greek, 'excuse me is your name Kariss?' She looked visibly relieved, 'yes I am Katina Kariss' she replied, sitting in one of the waiting room chairs.

There was another shattering crash and a disheveled male figure rushed in.

'Hello Angela, sorry I'm a bit late, please come into my surgery.'

His office was a large oak paneled room lined with boxes arranged in alphabetical order labeled - Albania, Angola, Belgium and so on right through the alphabet ending in Z starting with Zambia.

Knowing the doctor's weakness was traveling; I ventured, 'now where have you been recently?' What a mistake that was !

'I have just returned from Afghanistan, and would you believe it, of all places to get sick - that's where it happened. Actually I was in such a bad way they had to airlift me out of the country.'

'Oh my goodness,' I exclaimed — but there was more. 'The doctors in Turkey did an excellent job,' he continued.

'It certainly sounds as though you were very lucky,' I remarked.

Our client — Mrs Kariss moved restlessly, no doubt wondering what on earth was going on.

'When will he examine me?' she whispered in Greek squirming in her seat.

'The doctor talks yap, yap, but does nothing.'

'Oh don't worry I will remind him,' I assured her.

Dr Smedley was not to be put off, for he had found a willing listener. It was his duty to entertain his patient (who couldn't understand a word) — his friend the interpreter was bored stiff.

'Do you know about Afghanistan's history,' he asked.

'Oh no!' I thought. On and on he went although I tried to steer him back to the reason we were there.

Half an hour had elapsed, during which we received a non stop discourse on the history of Afghanistan and its socio-economic structure. Given the right time and place this may have been entertaining, but he had a patient who was there to be examined and I had another appointment to attend. Finally, after talking non - stop for nearly 30 minutes, he came to a halt.

'Well Mrs Gard it's been nice seeing you once again, please tell Mrs Kariss I will send a report to the insurance company,' he stopped, placing both palms on the desk.

At last I had a chance to respond, 'Dr Smedley you have given us a very interesting discourse on Afghanistan, but you have yet to examine the patient.'

Dr Smedley paused, clutching his head saying, 'Angela how right you are, I am so sorry, please apologize to Mrs Kariss — the poor lady, how silly of me.'

At this point the telephone rang, Dr Smedley answered it. 'I will not be a moment, please wait for me,' he said.

Turning to us he requested -

'Please ask Mrs Kariss to go into the examination room, and remove her dress — I will be with you in a moment.'

With that he rushed out of his office, and I heard him shout to Delia, 'I'll return shortly.'

Glancing out of the window I was just in time to see him climb into a gleaming silver Porsche "Targa" driven by a beautiful young blonde girl. The car roared off in a crackle of sporty exhaust and was gone.

Poor Mrs Kariss was standing in the examination room, wondering what to do next. 'Mrs Angeliky what is happening?' she cried.

'Mrs Kariss, I'm so sorry I have no idea — the doctor has disappeared,' I replied.

Leaving the office, I moved into the waiting room. 'Delia what do we do now,' I enquired.

'Angela, could I suggest you ask the patient to get dressed and I will try to get in contact with Dr Smedley,' she replied.

Mrs Kariss was furious. I was puzzled but not all that unhappy for my fee was guaranteed. Another 30 minutes elapsed, and as Dr Smedley had not returned I arranged another appointment with Delia and departed for my next job.

So ended the "art deco" story of the patient, the disappearing doctor and his travels in Afghanistan.

My next appointment had been arranged at the Preston Magistrates Court — it was a traffic matter concerning a lady by the name of Maria Demitriou. The contact at the police station was the Sergeant and Prosecutor James Morrison.

Parking my car, I walked across Bell Street, and up into Preston Police Station.

A tall policeman, who looked as though he was approaching seven feet tall, left his desk and confronted me at the counter.

'Oh thanks for coming, I'm Jim Morrison,' he said with a smile.

'Now how can I be of assistance,' I said.

'Well we have a lady here who doesn't speak much English.

She's about to front the Magistrate, having been "nicked" with her children driving down Foote Street Templestowe.

She was 30 kph over the speed limit.'

'Oh, I said, where is she, and is there any legal representation?'.

'To the best of my knowledge no — but a lack of Greek speakers makes things difficult.' Sergeant Morrison continued. 'Please follow me, she's outside the courthouse with a man I believe to be her husband.'

I followed the Sergeant to the front of the courthouse. Walking up to them I introduced myself in Greek. 'I am the independent interpreter provided to you by the police.'

Both of them stopped, 'the police will pay?' her husband asked looking at me enquiringly.

'Yes, that is correct,' I answered.

'Oh Mrs Angeliky, I was the driver, my name is Maria, she said -'this is my husband Chris, he's here to give me support.'

'Do you think I will go to the jail,' she asked clearly frightened.

'No you will not, but you might lose your drivers license,' I replied.

'But I was only going 30 klm over the limit, I did not know there was a speed limit in Foote St,' she cried.

'Do you have a solicitor?' I asked. 'No', she replied.

'Will you speak to the judge for me.'

'Yes, I replied, I will try and help you, but remember I am here to translate to the Magistrate exactly what is being said, and tell you how he responds. Come with me, and please put out your cigarettes, smoking in there is not allowed.'

We moved inside, taking our seats in the front of the court waiting for the magistrate to complete his paper work. After a nod from the clerk, the police prosecutor Jim Morrison arose clutching his notes.

He commenced by stating that Maria had been caught, driving frantically down Foote St, and had been booked for driving 30 klm over the limit.

'Now madam interpreter,' invited the Magistrate, 'would you please ask Mrs Dimitriou to step into the witness box, as I would like to hear her side of the story.'

Maria raised the bible in her left hand and I translated the oath to her.

'Please tell the magistrate exactly what happened Maria,' I instructed her.

She started slowly in Greek, while I interpreted what was said, a few sentences behind.

Apparently it was true that she was indeed driving 30 klm's over the speed limit, for she had been worried about her son's condition and was returning with him to the doctor.

The magistrate listened patiently, 'Madam interpreter, I am not going to waste time over this matter — normally the fine is $600 for the first offence and 9 months loss of license.

however, on the strength of the doctor's letter, I will fine your client $300 and suspend her drivers license for one month.'

Turning to Maria I explained the judges remarks. 'Mrs Angeliki please, this is a good man, ask him if he could find it in his heart to allow me to drive my children to school only between 7 and 8 am each morning?'

I did as she requested, and the magistrate's reaction was predictable.

He growled, 'tell Mrs Dimitriou I suggest she says no more, as I am seldom so lenient concerning matters of this nature.

Chapter 10

"The Man and the Ducks Affair"

The Owen Dixon Chambers is busy at the best of times, however close to 4 pm, cases were concluding, clerks run to and fro pushing trolleys bulging with files.

To add to the confusion, barristers clad in their black legal regalia complete with white horse hair wigs, scurry about, trying hard not to collide with each other.

On one such afternoon I joined a group of people, waiting at the lift door, trying to reach the floor of their choice in the shortest possible time. I noticed a short grey haired gentleman obviously Greek in the crowd join the group of patient passengers. As we entered, the lift doors closed with a soft thud and slowly ascended.

At the 5th level the door opened with a soft "hiss" and I stepped outside followed by the passenger I described.

We were both heading to Room 612 - the chambers of Andrew Steele - Barrister of Law.

The grey haired, bearded, bewigged and gowned figure of Andrew Steele looked up from his desk as we entered. Then I realized the man following me must be my client — one by the name of Athanasios Bourkas.

Looking at me Bourkas remarked, ' is your surname is Gard?'

I replied that it was correct.

'I'm married to an Australian.' 'Oh never mind,' he said, looking at me with a really sad expression on his face. 'What do you mean never mind', I responded in Greek.

Sensing that I was more than a little offended he shook his head scratching his jaw. 'It's okay if he's a good man.' I didn't reply as many Greek's with whom I associate migrated to Australia for a better life in the early 60s.

At that time the language was a problem.

Misunderstandings were commonplace — thus families preferred their children to marry into the Greek community preserving the language, customs and culture.

After introductions were made and we were seated, Steele asked me to request Athanasios to tell his story — as he did, I started translating.

It commenced with details of the problem – how Athanasios had traveled to Bolac the night prior to the start of the Duck Hunting Season, armed with two shotguns, a heap of cartridges and a valid shot gun license.

Being a relative newcomer to our shores he was totally unaware that the "license" permitted him to shoot only certain species of wildfowl – consequently he blasted away at anything flying at that time of the morning. The resulting "barrage" dispatched 16 species of protected water fowl to that "great lagoon in the sky."

Steele nodded sympathetically. 'Oh yes - now I can understand the problem let me think as to how we best tackle it!'

'Now my man,' he said looking straight at us, 'please Mrs Gard - this is most important.

I want him to understand that owing to the Courts location, it will be impossible for me to attend. However I am happy to place this matter in the capable hands of a colleague of mine in Geelong who is more than able to handle this matter.

Athanasios looked at me, obviously disappointed when I translated what had been said.

'Mrs Angeliky, he said in Greek, please tell this man that if he is unable, I understand — so long as who he recommends is a good man to represent me.'

'Please excuse me a moment,' Steele said reaching for the telephone. I'm going to phone my colleague in Geelong to ascertain whether or not he's available.'

'May I speak to Paul Allan please?' he rasped into the telephone.

'Oh Paul, this is Andrew Steele – how are things down in your "neck of the woods?" I see – well that's good news – anyway the reason for my call is to see whether you're available for a job down at the Bolac Magistrates Court on the 23rd.

Great – I have an Athanasios Bourkas who is in trouble with the "powers that be", on account of having blown some locally protected wild fowl into the "hereafter."

The local Gendarmes and the Anti- Gun Alliance to make matters worse took a dim view of such "goings on" and ensured he was arrested.

Now taking into account that a knowledge of the Greek language is not one of your skills, I have arranged an interpreter (Angeliky Gard) to attend in order to sort out any possible difficulties.

Good — I'm glad, okay I can leave them in your capable hands.'

'Mrs Gard could you explain to Mr Bourkas - in case he is still a little puzzled exactly what is going on. He must turn up at the Bolac Magistrates Court on or before 9.30 am on the 23rd of this month. It will be necessary to meet Paul Allan, my colleague, to participate in a brief conference beforehand. Although the Court starts at 10 am he is required to arrive early to facilitate this.'

With that, the meeting ended abruptly, so I sat with him in the foyer and explained as I had been instructed.

I left by car early on the appointed morning, and after a quick cup of coffee in Geelong, resumed my journey. At 10 am it was necessary to meet my client Athanasios Boukas, together with his solicitor, for us to hold a conference before court.

The magistrates court in the tiny town of Bolac was not hard to find. The main street had everything from the local undertaker to the police station, and a forlorn structure next door — yes there it was the Bolac magistrates court, an example of decaying Victorian architecture forming part of a rural township (population 1529), set amid rolling grassy plains, some 140 kilometers west of Melbourne.

The weather had changed, a cold westerly howled down the main street, a small group of people stood outside court house shivering — both in anticipation of their cases and as a result of the freezing weather.

I arrived at 9.30 am, parked near the court house, locked my car and set out to find my clients. Suddenly I spotted them. Our solicitor – Paul Allan must be the tall grey haired gentleman carrying a bundle of files bound in pink tape, trying to talk to the same short dark man smoking frantically, by the look of it to calm his nerves.

The howling wind clutched at my coat ruffling my hair as I moved over to meet him. 'Good morning, I'm Angeliky Gard the Greek interpreter,' I introduced myself to the person I surmised to be the solicitor Paul Allan.

'Oh I am pleased to meet you Angeliky, I believe you have met our client Athanasios Bourkas. I'm Paul Allan,' he said. I extended my hand and he shook it. 'Perhaps we could check exactly what you have discussed with Mr Buxton,' he suggested. 'Well Mrs Gard, it appears we have quite a problem. Athanasios shot wild ducks belonging to an endangered species and was caught in the act. To make matters, the local "gendarmes" who arrested him are of course responsible for who shoots who and what around here and on Lake Bolac. As it turned out Mr Bourkas' "brush with the law" became heated, partly as a result of the language question, and because of the Anti - Gun Alliance who had made their presence felt.

They delight in leaving no stone unturned to ensure that the relevant authority knew all about it. To cut a long story short, he was arrested and subsequently "bailed", still protesting he had no idea why he had been treated in this manner.'

When I explained to him the implications and that the law in Australia takes a dim view of their protected bird species being shot, he looked at me sheepishly, gravely nodding his head when asked if the charge was true. 'I go shooting in the Greece, - shrugging his shoulders, there's no problem — plenty more ducks,' he replied in Greek.

'Yes I said, that is correct, but don't forget you are in another country and there are laws in Australia which prohibit you from shooting certain species of wild birds.'

He shrugged his shoulders in a characteristically Greek fashion and proceeded to turn yet another cigarette into glowing ash.

I said to Mr Allan — 'I understand what has happened, you see in Greece it is considered a sign of "manhood" to go shooting. No doubt the reason there is a notable absence of wild birds is the relaxed attitude to the subject.

In the past they used to blast away at all and sundry until recentl recently.' I suggested to Allan the crux of the matter was the question of "cultural difference" and Athanasios inability to understand the English language & local customs..

'Yes Angeliky, I agree, replied Allan. The question of the "cultural difference" is a good one upon which we can base our plea.'

The weather conditions were appalling — rain was driven almost horizontally by the bitterly cold west wind as it swept down the almost deserted main street. 'I am so cold, I said.— 'what about if we adjourn to inside the court house and continue our discussion in there.'

My client and his solicitor were quick to agree.

The Bolac Magistrates Court had seen better days. Actually it was built in the "horse and buggy era" when the pace of life was more leisurely. The topic in those days centered around Australia's participation in the Boer War, then the First World War, later the latest price of wheat and wool. The city fathers had decided to erect this then — imposing structure to relieve the constabulary of the odious task of transferring the local miscreants in a horse drawn "Black Mariah" to Geelong for their hearing. With the building of the court house, Bolac "became of age", and cases were heard by the circuit judge during one of his periodic visits to the town.

Many years had passed however since those days. Bolac, along with most rural towns, remembered those who lost their lives in bygone wars, erecting an imposing monument in their main street to those soldiers of the era.

True to the custom Bolac was no exception.

A large white painted memorial was located at the junction where the main street was intersected by the road west. Here the obligatory concrete soldier dressed in Boer War uniform was blowing a silent reveille into a howling gale. Little else had been done to the court building, apart from the occasional coat of paint. It remained much the same as it was in earlier days - apart from one concession to progress — the connection of electricity.

One cheerful aspect of the otherwise bleak paneled court room, was a huge hearth in which a cheery log fire snapped and crackled, casting a rosy glow upon proceedings.

Deciding to maximize the warmth, we chose our seats as close as we could to the fire. High above towered the magistrates desk (or throne as it initially appeared). Seated in a commanding position was a white haired bespectacled gentleman in his late sixties dressed in a thick woolen overcoat and scarf. He sat there writing away frantically, occasionally peering over the top of his "half moon" type spectacles balanced half way down a long pointed nose. His assistant or clerk, similarly attired, sat below him, sifting through a huge pile of legal paperwork.

'Your Worship, the next case is the Crown verses Bourkas,' announced his clerk.

'Can we proceed?' 'Oh very well, replied the magistrate. Will you call them please.'

Before the clerk had time to respond, our solicitor was on his feet.

'Your Worship, my name is Paul Allan, I am appearing on behalf of the plaintiff. My client's English is somewhat limited, we have engaged an interpreter. It's the lady on my right – Angeliky Gard.' Taking this to be my cue, I stood and bowed to the magistrate.

Peering down from his lofty perch he grumbled, 'really Mr Allan is all this necessary? According to the statement I am reading there's little doubt your client was responsible for what occurred, eh!'

That morning, the judge appeared distinctly "unwell"; perhaps his activities on the previous evening had had a direct influence on his current humor — or lack of it.

I regained my seat, Paul Allan was on his feet once again.

'Your Worship I can appreciate the way you are thinking. However there are a number of aspects about this case that need to be brought to your attention by using our interpreter.

As the "matter" proceeds you will better understand the position.'

The magistrate grunted his approval, and recommended writing, saying without raising his head. 'Who's prosecuting? he growled'

'I am your Worship. My name is Constable Reid of Bolac Police. It's my duty to ensure that the regulations concerning the question of firearm registration and shooters licenses are adhered to, together with the protection of certain waterfowl.'

'I see, responded the magistrate. Well before we start, were his firearm and shooters documents valid and up to date?'

'Yes your Worship,' responded the constable.

'Well at least that's a start,' ventured the magistrate. 'Very well then, Constable Reid please enter the witness box and take the oath.'

The constable clomped up the stairs. Taking the Bible in his right hand he proceeded to do as requested.

The magistrate looked directly across at him.

'Kindly acquaint the Court as to the exact circumstances surrounding the offence.'

'Constable Reid commenced, referring periodically to the pages of a blue notebook (government issue) intoning in a flat monotone. 'I visited Lake Bolac at 5 am on the 5th of April last in order to check firearm documents and try to "keep the peace" between the shooters and folk from the Antigun Alliance who had attended in force. I stopped the "accused," checked his documentation which as I have stated was in order. When I requested to examine his bag, Mr Bourkas became agitated but eventually cooperated. Inside I discovered he had shot sixteen protected waterfowl.

When it was explained to the accused, he shrugged his shoulders, zipped up his bag and attempted to push past us. At that stage we had no option other than to arrest him.'

The magistrate appeared puzzled. 'Constable Reid — how did you communicate with the accused as he speaks little or no English?'

'Your Worship, unfortunately we were not in a position to do this, as no one speaks Greek,' replied the policeman.

'Mr. Allan, in light of this would you like to cross examine the witness,' suggested the magistrate.

Paul Allan was on his feet in a flash, for the magistrate had handed the verdict to him on a silver platter.

'Constable Reid —' he commenced. 'Please explain to the magistrate just how it was possible for you to obtain his shooters license and firearm registration papers when the poor man obviously had no idea what you and your colleague where up to?'

The constable became very uneasy, shifting nervously from one foot to the other in the witness box.

'My colleague and I apprehended the accused, searched him and found the paper work we needed.'

Mr. Paul Allan commenced to mount his attack.

'In other words when it came to the question of the bag - firstly you arrested him in order to conduct a forced search, with the poor man having no idea why he was being treated in such a disrespectful manner. He thought you were out to steal his birds!

In view of the circumstances it is hardly surprising that he showed resistance.'

The magistrate suddenly started to realize it was not an "open and shut case," for indeed there were two aspects, both of which needed closer examination.

'Thank you Mr Allan, the position is becoming clearer.- do you have anything further to ask the witness? If not, I would like you to call Mr Bourkas together with his interpreter into the witness box.'

I took this as my cue to lead a very nervous client up those creaky old stairs. Taking the Bible in my right hand I recited the Interpreters oath. Handing the Bible to Athanasios Bourkas I asked him to repeat the oath which I interpreted into Greek.

He did so, stumbling verbally through nervousness.

When we concluded I addressed the magistrate. 'Your Worship our client wishes to make a statement to explain what has happened.'

'Very well madam interpreter, please proceed,' cooed the judge.

As Bourkas spoke, I commenced interpreting the dialogue. 'Our client says that he arrived from Greece only twelve months ago. Since his arrival he has been trying to establish himself in this country. In Greece there is no such protection for the wild birds — all are regarded as "fair game" and hunted as such. He was surprised therefore to be forcibly detained by the Police who he thought were trying to steal his birds.'

The magistrate looked surprised and muttered. 'Please thank Mr Bourkas for me madam interpreter. If there is nothing further from the police, you can both leave the witness box.'

As we clambered down those creaky wooden stairs I was wondering if the theories espoused by those advocating the multi cultural society had reached Bolac?

In his summation, the magistrate found: 'Though ignorance of the law is no excuse for what has occurred, I understand the circumstances the plaintiff found himself in.

'As a result I have decided not to record a conviction, however he is required to make a donation of $100 to the "poor box". Before concluding however I place on record my displeasure at the heavy handed tactics employed by the police. I draw to their attention the existence of the telephone interpreter service operating to ensure that misunderstandings of this nature do not occur — case dismissed!'

The police, looking decidedly unhappy, left immediately.

As ours was the final case in his court, the magistrate beckoned to me. I moved closer to his lofty perch.

'Mrs.Gard, personally I am very fond of wild fowl. Could you please ask your client what he likens the taste of the "blue spotted wood duck" to?'

'Certainly your Worship ' I replied and motioned to Bourkas, who moved towards me apprehensively. I asked him in Greek. 'The magistrate is interested in the taste of the bird you shot — what would you liken it to?'

He looked thoughtful, stroking his chin before replying in Greek — please tell the magistrate it tasted somewhere between a swan and a kookaburra.

'Have you shot these types of birds before?' I gasped.

'Of course,' he replied —

I was thunderstruck, these birds are also protected species. Unused as I am to "thinking on my feet," I had to produce a response that would satisfy the magistrate, as I had no wish to see Bourkas land himself in further hot water.

I responded with, 'Your Worship, Mr Bourkas says the taste is somewhere between lamb and kangaroo.'

'Thank you Mrs Gard,' he replied, his curiosity apparently satisfied.

Fortunately being slightly deaf, he had not fully understood Bourkas response, for although in Greek, he had used two English words — "swan and kookaburra."

Paul Allan was delighted with the result and as we left the court house he asked, 'Angeliky what did the magistrate ask you?' I replied, 'what the bird tasted like — our friend here answered by saying it was somewhere between a swan and a kookaburra.'

Paul Allan turned pale. 'How did you respond to his question?'

'Oh don't worry, I replied, I thought quickly and told him it tasted somewhere between lamb and kangaroo!'

'Well done Angeliky,' he replied.

Come with me and I'll buy you a coffee before he gets us into any more strife!'

Chapter 11

"The Man and the miracle"

'Hi Angeliky, this is Grace,' said a voice at the other end of the phone.

'Here is your list of appointments for next week. Last but not least, there is one on Friday, it's at the Workers Compensation Board — there will be a conference before the hearing.

The client's name is Spiros Petropoulos, he has a back injury and is seeking compensation.'

Fridays are a good day for me — the end of the working week. I reasoned I'd be able to wrap this job up by lunchtime, and do my shopping at Victoria Market on the way home.

Victoria Market is the largest fruit, vegetable and meat market in Melbourne. It was established during the reign of Queen Victoria, remaining unchanged since those days.

Approaches have been made by developers to erect a multi storied hotel complex on the site, however they had all been rejected owing to a union black ban, insisting that — "This is the peoples' market, and should remain as such."

Friday dawned, (the weather in March is perfect), the temperature about 23 degrees, with clouds suspended like balls of cotton wool, in the clear blue sky. The traffic was relatively light, so I had no problem in parking.

Up in the lift I went, and stepped out onto Bourke Street.

The huge plane trees which line this Champs d' Elysee of Melbourne were in full leaf, filtering the dappled sunlight which created moving patterns on the pavement.

The Workers Compensation Board, was housed in a large concrete and glass edifice soaring some twenty stories up into the heavens. Most of the building is occupied by one of the major banks, the rest by the offices of the Small Claims Tribunal, together with the Workers Compensation Board. Riding in the lift some sixteen stories above Bourke St, the doors opened softly to reveal the Workers Compensation Board's reception area, and my hunt began to locate my client Mr Petropoulos, and his barrister Ian Anderson.

I was immediately successful.

Seated near the receptionist, and looking very self conscious was a small dark haired man in his early thirties, accompanied by a middle aged thickset man clutching a large bundle of (what looked like) legal papers.

I approached them slowly, introducing myself.

My client was delighted that I had arrived — as he was having difficulty understanding what was happening. Additionally, he was having a problem standing, which he only able to do so with the aid of a walking stick.

Ian Anderson knocked on a conference room door, opened it and ushered us inside 'Mrs Gard, perhaps I should give you some background to this case,' he suggested.

'Before the accident, Mr Petropoulos was a process worker out at the GMH factory in Dandenong. Apparently while fitting an engine he slipped, injuring his back. After a long period of treatment and numerous doctors reports, the problem does not appear to be getting any better.

If anything, the injury seemed to be worsening. I noticed that Petropoulos looked extremely unwell, leaning heavily on his walking stick. At Anderson's request, I asked my client whether he could do any further work to earn a living.

'No', he replied, he had been relying on sickness benefits.

'Okay Mrs Gard, let's go over how the accident occurred,' said Anderson.

'Can you explain to me, the exact sequence of events which led to your injury?' I asked him in Greek.

Mr Petropoulos drew a deep breath and commenced, half in Greek and half English.

'One day after the lunch time, I was lifting an engine block with two other men, it was very heavy, I slipped hurting my back.' His right hand moved behind him, touching the alleged damaged area.

'How long has he been in this condition?' asked Anderson, nodding sympathetically.

I asked in Greek and he replied. 'Me like this for the past four years,' I translated for Mr. Petropoulos, while a mournful expression spread across his face.

'Where is his wife, is she here?' asked Anderson.

'She's not well, she's not here today,' I translated on the client's behalf.

'Okay, could you ask him to detail how this has affected the physical side of his married life. Anderson paused and started again, appearing embarrassed, 'Ah - I mean his sex life', he said, staring at the table and writing faster.

Oh, I thought, I knew that part was coming!

I translated the question and awaited the answer. Tears welled in his eyes, his shoulders shook for he was only too anxious to tell us all the details in color and full stereophonic sound.

He left us in no doubt that the accident had damaged that part of his anatomy which was beyond repair. In short, he was a ruined man.

'So your wife is still with you in spite of everything?' queried Mr Anderson.

'Yes, she's a good woman,' replied Mr Petropoulos.

'What figure did his solicitor put on the question of compensation? I don't seem to find it in here,' said Anderson rummaging through his papers. So I asked him, 'what was the compensation figure you discussed?'

'Solicitor said $100,000, but I want my health,' he replied.

'Umm that's a lot of money,' replied Anderson, 'are you sure about that figure?' Petropoulos confirmed the amount.

'Okay, let's see what we can do, I will speak to the opposition, maybe we can come up with a satisfactory arrangement for him.'

Mr Petropoulos was inconsolable; he cried for his wife, his job, his house and his future, as far as he was concerned his life had been ruined.

Time went by - no Ian Anderson. In desperation I opened the door of the conference room and looked outside. Anderson was in the corridor, and by his expression I knew there was not going to be a "quick fix."

'Mrs Gard please tell him to prepare himself. The opposition's attitude has not shifted, for they will not even consider making us an offer. I cannot understand it, as from past experience, there is always room to negotiate. It makes me wonder just what they have up their sleeve,' he shook his head and sat down looking quite depressed.

When I translated our conversation, Mr. Petropoulos looked even glummer.

A bright pair I've got here, I thought, envisaging the prospect of my Friday afternoon's shopping expedition fading over the horizon.

'I think we had better go outside, we won't hear anything in here if we are called,' said Ian Anderson moving to open the door.

I assisted Mr.Petropolous as he tottered along, as the public address system announced 'Petropoulos, Court room 17.'

Court room 17 used green as its predominant colour. The walls were painted in a lime green, the judges' chairs were covered in a dark green leather - while seating in the body of the court was upholstered in a woven green fabric. The only concession to this monopoly of colour was a huge multicolored Victorian coat of arms (which appeared to be made from paper mache) adorning the wall, and the grey carpet which bore the Victorian crest woven into the pile.

We were shown to our seats by an usher, who checked that all parties in the case were present. There was a rustle of clothing, the three judges who were to hear the case entered.

They bowed, we bowed, taking our places in the body of the court. The judges shuffled their piles of paper until one thin balding gentleman raised his head.

'Now, who have we appearing for the plaintiff?' he questioned.

'I am your honor, my name is Ian Anderson and I am appearing on behalf of the Plaintiff - Petropoulos', ventured Anderson. 'I appear for the Newhaven Insurance Company the defendants in this matter - my name is Andrew Stewart,' added a thickset younger man.

Ian Anderson addressed the judges, explaining the details of the case.

Taking the Bible in my right hand, I declared the interpreters oath, then as I stood by my client a door opened and someone entered the rear of the court room.

Suddenly our client turned grey — beads of perspiration broke out on his forehead. He spoke to me in Greek saying, 'outside, I must talk to you outside.' I looked over to the barrister and beckoned to him - 'he wants to talk to us outside.' Anderson requested that we adjourn for five minutes — the judges reluctantly agreed.

I noticed a remarkable transformation had taken place. Spiro moved quite rapidly out of the witness box, leading the way to the corridor outside. He said to me, obviously very frightened : 'That man who came in while I was in the witness box, is my current boss,' he said visibly shaking - panic was written all over his face.

'He is my boss, I have been working since the accident, I lied' —
he told me in Greek.

Before I had a chance to interpret his remarks to a puzzled Ian
Anderson, our "crippled" client had thrown away his stick, and was
running for his life toward the lift doors, which closed swallowing him
with a soft thud. I had witnessed a miraculous cure take place. From the
stories I have heard since, the Workers Compensation Board may one
day be known as the "Lourdes of Melbourne", for here within these
august premises, "miracles" are not at all uncommon!

Chapter 12

"The Man and the Fur Coat"

The wind howled through the trees bending them nearly to the ground.- the rain was being driven almost horizontal, causing the Volvo's wipers to work overtime clearing the excess water. The weather was so bad the bird population around Tullamarine airport were prompted to walk instead of fly. As I approached the airport, twinkling lights in the sky signified that I was not the only person mad enough to endure these conditions.

Entering the car park I was accosted by a rather officious uniformed gentleman who was sitting in his warm gate house, until I rudely interrupted his solitude.

'Just a moment young lady,' (this was rather flattering for a woman with two children).

He blinked and looked again, 'sorry Madam, you can't park here,' he said.

I thought why are little men, particularly parking officers in uniform, always so officious?

'Yes I can, I am the Greek interpreter requested by Jim Reynolds of the Department of Customs - he has directed me to this car park', I responded.

Unused to being challenged, he looked at me closely, apparently impressed by my forth right response. He blinked again. 'Oh okay, would you please stay where you are?

I'll get clearance from management.' He returned to the gate house, dialed a number and spoke for several minutes before returning the handset to its cradle. 'Okay Mrs Gard (at least he had that part right), I would like you to park over there, to the right near the door marked Customs Entrance.'

'Thank you very much for your assistance,' I replied as he waved me through, rather like a controller on the deck of the aircraft carrier "Ark Royal" parking aircraft.

Once inside the terminal building, the atmosphere became distinctly warmer. I removed my coat at the linoleum topped counter in the section marked Customs & Excise.

I rang the bell - nothing happened. After a wait of some two minutes, I rang once again.

Finally there were vague stirrings from behind a grey screen at the centre of the office.

Some three minutes later a stout white haired man ambled sleepily toward me.

Jim Reynolds introduced himself and sat me down to explain the purpose of my visit to Tullamarine. Smuggling has always been a major problem for the Australian Customs.

It not only costs our government revenue, but it poses other dangerous risks. Apparently my country folk often try to introduce plants to supplement their own gardens. Although this practice seems innocent enough, it presents a free ride for diseases from Europe and other countries.

'Tonight the aircraft we are targeting is the Olympic Airlines flight from Athens arriving at about 2300 hrs.' (11 pm).

I sat in the office and waited – OA 471 arrived at exactly 11.25 pm.

Yes, I thought, this reflects the typically relaxed Grecian attitude as to being on time.

I guess owing to the bad weather they had a good excuse. The first trickle of people made their way from the aircraft and moved through passport control, then into the main baggage area and the luggage carousels. After a short delay the carousels started to produce a long line of multi colored suitcases. I sat intrigued, watching the processing of the jumbo jet full of people on the customs department television monitors. Then the telephone rang and Jim Reynolds said, 'right, it looks as though we have your first "customer" ready and waiting - we have a lady who has not declared a fur coat.'

'Really,' I said, 'is this where the fun begins?'

'Yes, he replied, and the lady is not at all happy.'

I followed him into the baggage hall, and out through a side door to another room which bore a sign — Interview Room 3.

The room was furnished with a desk and four chairs while the illumination was provided by a recessed florescent light which cast a blinding white glow over the scene.

'Please take a seat Mrs Gard, said Jim Reynolds — shortly an officer will be in to conduct the passenger interview.'

There was a loud knock at the door, and a woman in her early fifties was escorted inside.

She was wearing a huge white fur coat (which made her look like a polar bear) — escorted by another Customs and Excise Officer; this time female, by the name of Margaret Barnes.

After the introductions – Jim left the room.

Officer Barnes requested, 'would you ask the lady to take a seat and remove her coat in order that I can examine it?'

I introduced myself and asked for her coat. 'do I have to? she asked. The weather outside is freezing.'

'The air conditioning in here is excellent, and this lady wants to examine your coat.'

'Oh very well,' she snorted removing the bulky garment and draping it over the desk.

Margaret Barnes commenced. 'Now Mrs Mantzos, where have you come from?'

'I have come from Athens,' Flora Mantzos replied in Greek which I hurriedly translated.

'Yes, I know that, but what parts of Greece have you visited during your stay in that country,' insisted Officer Barnes.

Flora pursed her lips, 'I want to go home to my family - why do you keep me here?

Call my husband,' she demanded in Greek.

I replied, 'look, the sooner you answer the questions, the sooner we can all finish.

Now, please answer the question.'

She sighed, and continued, 'we went to Salonica, Larissa, and Florina, where I stayed with my sister.'

'I see,' said Officer Barnes picking up the coat and examining the label.

Mrs Mantzos where did you buy this coat?,' she asked.

Mrs Mantzos looked thoughtful, 'my husband bought it in Australia,' she replied.

'Okay Mrs Gard, would you kindly examine the label and tell me what it says,'

requested Officer Barnes.

I reached over and translated. 'Made in Greece and sold by Papadopoulos Bros Kastoria.- Greece.'

'Would you have the receipt Mrs Mantzos?' asked Officer Barnes.

'No of course I haven't, my husband bought the coat for me as a surprise,' she replied.

'Okay then, I will detain you no longer. Here is a receipt for the garment, it will be kept in safe keeping until the country of original purchase can be proved,' said Margaret Barnes handing her a Customs receipt and taking the coat.

Mrs Mantzos erupted, 'you thief, you all crooks,' she shouted hysterically in Greek, fearing that this would be the last she would see of her coat.

'Mrs Mantzos, please restrain yourself,' I said in Greek. 'Remember these people are like the police and can arrest you if you misbehave. The correct thing to do is go home now and find the shop receipt, to reclaim your coat'

She grabbed the Custom's receipt and stormed out of the room in tears.

'What was all that about?' inquired Margaret Barnes.

'She's upset,' I replied, and is going home to find the proof you require.'

'Why would someone take a fur coat to Greece, which is experiencing one of the hottest summers on record? The coat is brand new from Kastoria in Northern Greece, the home of the Greek fur trade, and according to the label, that is where the coat has been made and sold.

I'm sure that's where it was purchased. Anyway, we will see if and when she contacts us,' said Margaret Barnes smiling. We have another one. He speaks no English, and he says that he has nothing to declare, however we think otherwise.'

The door flew open with a "bang", and an overweight, balding customs officer followed one of my countrymen — a bearded man with two days growth and wearing disheveled clothing.

He was very upset and frightened.

Bill Peach, the customs officer, took over from Margaret. He introduced me to Spiro Katsos, before lowering himself into the chair which squeaked in protest, and commenced.

'Could you ask Mr Katsos how long he has been in Greece,' he asked.

'Why does he ask me that - I do not ask him how much he weighs,' responded the frustrated Spiro in Greek.

'We can leave here quickly if you answer the questions correctly. If you don't answer the questions we will be here all night, I replied in Greek.— it's up to you.'

'I was in Greece for two months,' he snorted..

Bill Peach awoke, 'what did he say?'

I repeated, that he had been in Greece for two months.

'Okay, now where did he stay in Greece,' he asked and I repeated that he stayed in his brother's house in Tripolis.'

'What part of Greece is Tripolis in,' asked the puzzled Officer Peach.

'Oh, I don't have to translate that one. It's a large town in Northern Peleponnese,' I replied.

'What type of farming does his brother take part in?' asked Officer Peach.

'Why is the "hondros" (fatso) asking me all these questions?' Katsos responded in Greek. I raised my hand and stopped him.

'Really Mr Spiro, do you want to be here all night?'

He reluctantly explained that his brother Athanasios had a vineyard and a few sheep.

That seemed to be the extent of the questioning from Officer Peach:

'Mrs Gard would you ask Mr Katsos to bring in his luggage — I want to examine his bags.'

Katsos snorted his frustration 'can't he get off his big fat "colo" (bottom) and help!'

Katsos stopped when I held up my hand, I was so annoyed by his outburst I felt like hitting him.

The first case entered the room and landed on Officer Peach's desk with a thud.

Peering over the top of the huge suitcase, Officer Peach looked Spiros straight in the eye, saying, 'Mrs Gard I want to be fair. Please ask him if he has read the Australian Customs Regulations over there on the wall,' he said pointing to the notice in Greek.

'Now for the last time, does he have anything to declare?' asked Bill Peach.

'No I have nothing to declare,' Mr Spiro replied angrily.

I asked him to open the cases. He did so, and an overpowering smell of unwashed clothing flooded the room. Officer Peach parted the seemingly solid mass, carefully placing each article to one side. Reaching the shoes he felt inside one. Then, like a magician pulling a rabbit out of a hat, he produced a bundle of cuttings packed in plastic.

'Well now Mr Katsos, what have we here, he said with a satisfied gleam in his eye.

I thought you said you have nothing to declare.'

'Would you ask him what his explanation is for this and if there is anything else?'

Mr Spiros' face fell. 'Oh my brother, will get me into trouble. I did not know of this please believe me,' he whimpered in Greek, his face turned pale as the Customs Officer started to dig even deeper.

'Oh, now, what's this?' he cried gleefully, removing a large jar of a suspiciously anonymous orange goo.

'Let me have a look at that,' I said removing the cap, smelling it cautiously.

'I have not seen that for years — I ventured, my Grandmother used to make it, it's a face cream made from yoghurt and herbs.'

'Okay, that seems innocent enough' said Bill poking around in the orange goo with the end of a blue ballpoint pen to ensure nothing sinister lurked inside.

'Goodness, fancy anyone putting that muck on their face,' he remarked with a smile.

Every shoe he removed contained cuttings, carefully wrapped in plastic. It appeared he had enough to plant a vineyard.

'Please explain Mrs Gard that it is an offence under the Customs and Excise Act to bring in vine cuttings. They can ruin our agriculture, in particular the wine industry, if the cuttings are carrying any disease.'

Two hours later, I emerged from the interview room exhausted. Apparently Mr Spiro could expect a fine of at least $500. He clearly knew of the regulations yet had decided not to declare his future vineyard. Fortunately that was not my worry.

I collected my car, turned off onto the Tullamarine Freeway once more, and headed South East into the night for home and a nice warm bed, imaging Spiro explaining to his family that their plans to make a fortune from the vineyard had been thwarted by this lady who hailed from the Peleponnese!

Chapter 13

"The Man and his Princess"

When my services were requested to assist with an insurance investigation out at Broadmeadows, I was at first reluctant to accept the job. It is located on the Hume highway in a light industrial area about as far north as you can travel, before suburbia gives way to the real countryside en route to Sydney.

The night before I worked out a detailed plan as to how I would reach my destination.

so early one morning I set off armed with my plan and street directory.

Just prior to Easter the weather in Melbourne can change from a daily average of 23 degrees with clear blue skies to rain and gale force winds — these conditions give Victoria the reputation of presenting three seasons in one day.

Today was one of those typical March days, as damp and miserable as it could get.

Driving along Bell Street Preston to the start of the Tullamarine Freeway — then out along Pascoe Vale Rd, the rain hammered the car. Being unfamiliar with this part of Melbourne, I carefully drove north as names of unknown suburbs flashed past.

After what seemed an eternity I was confronted by a huge sign declaring "Welcome to the City of Broadmeadows". Oh good! I thought. With a large shopping centre on my left, I pulled over to consult my street directory seeking reassurance. After carefully studying the map, I navigated my way through the flat rain drenched outer suburban streets, until the scenery changed abruptly. There was sign announcing "Arnold Rd", which bisected a light industrial estate of small factories — all of which had seen better days.

'So far so good,' I thought, stopping outside one large building number 23 — a large sign proclaiming to all it was the head office of "Hellenic Kitchens Pty Ltd".

Parking my car, I noticed the presence of a red BMW sedan stationary in the car park.

This must be the insurance investigator, I thought, feeling more confident, as there was no one in sight. At that moment — the heavens opened, and the rain tumbled down. Stepping out of my car, I locked the door and ran for cover straight to Hellenic Kitchen's factory front door.

I announced my arrival by knocking briskly. There was the sound of scurrying footsteps and the grey steel lined door swung open. A tall grey haired man clad in bib and brace overalls, sporting a huge moustache, stood before me. 'Good morning, my name is Angeliky Gard,' I announced in English. *'Nay*, he responded in Greek — *moment'* he said disappearing back into the bowels of the building.

A few moments later a short balding man dressed in a blue pin stripped suit emerged.

'Ah, hello, are you Angeliky Gard the Greek interpreter,' he asked?

'Yes indeed I am,' I replied.

'Oh, please come inside before you're drowned. I'm Alexander Rodgers the insurance investigator,' he said shaking my hand.

Turning, he introduced the mustachioed gentleman standing behind him, 'Angeliky please meet your client, Peter Alexapoulos.'

'Peter, this lady is your interpreter, Angeliky Gard,' he said in English.

Peter stood back thoughtfully stroking his moustache.

'Ah, he observed, *good* me learn a new English word today — *terpreter*.'

'Well Angeliky, come with me and we will conduct the interview in his office,'

Alexander suggested.

It seemed that saw dust cloaked everything, it covered the floor, lay all over the desks and chairs, and blanketed the account books.

'Okay, please take a seat,' suggested Alexander as he dusted a chair for me.' We'll try to get things rolling.'

'Thank your Mr Rodgers, but before we commence, could you please give me some idea as to what has occurred,' I asked.

Rodgers sighed thoughtfully.

'Well as far as we can ascertain, it's a combined motor vehicles claim of some $96,000. There were three vehicles involved, one of which belonged to the "guilty party" — our client Peter. His Datsun ZX 200 Sports was a complete "write off" together with two other vehicles owned by his neighbors. At this stage could you perhaps get his side of the story,' he requested.

As I had discussed these matters in English, my client "Peter", became increasingly curious and was relieved when I turned to him asking in Greek for his version.

'Mrs Angela, he responded. 'I had some money because I work hard that I decided to buy myself a Datsun sports car, you see; he continued drawing himself up to full height. I see the Lebanese, they drive Mercedes, the Turkish they drive the BMW, I said to myself, Peter you work hard so you deserve something that will please you.'

I explained the gist of the conversation to Alexander, who was tapping away furiously on his laptop computer. Pausing for a moment he remarked — 'Angeliky, would you ask him please just as a matter of interest, does he own any other vehicle.'

I did so, and awaited his response.

'Mrs Angela, please tell the man, I brought my wife "Tarago", you see,' he swept his hand around in an arc, pointing at a family photograph. 'I buy the car for her as after four boys, my wife she produce for me a girl, my little Princess,' his eyes shone and he knocked on the desk with his knuckles to accentuate his delight and pride at the birth of his daughter.

Alexander looked startled, so I stopped him and explained the gesture.

'Oh I see, it must have been quite a relief for his wife after so many boys,' Alexander remarked smiling.

I decided not to respond with a laugh as Peter might misinterpret my reaction.

Switching the conversation to the demise of his sports car I asked him.

'Now Peter can you tell me about your car and exactly what happened.'

'I wanted a sports car with plenty of "brmm brmm", you know Mrs Angela. Fortunately, before I left, the salesman, he signed me up with an insurance policy — he was a good man. It cost a lot of money but I'm so glad he insisted that I took it out.'

Before he could draw breath – I had translated the story thus far to Alexander.

Stopping he asked, 'Angeliky, could you ask him the amount of money he owes on the two vehicles.'

When I asked him how much he owed the bank for the vehicles, he was horrified.

'Mrs Angela I do not trust banks, if I buy anything like that I pay "cashie." With that he took me by the arm saying, 'look at this I show you.' With that he bent down and opened a green metal sliding drawer of the office filing cabinet. He removed a container covered by a red velvet cloth and unwrapped it. From his pocket he produced a key and opened the box.

I gasped in amazement for inside was an absolute treasure trove of money, thousands of dollars, neatly packaged.

'Now I understand what you mean, I said — you have your own bank.'

'Really Angeliky, I wish he had not shown us all this money, please advise him to put it in a bank,' advised Alexander. I wish he had not shown us all this money.'

Poor Alexander was really shocked, I don't think he had ever seen so much money in one spot in all his life.

To clear the air, I decided to ask him to recount the rest of the story as he had only got as far as the salesman arranging the insurance.

'Okay Mrs Angela I will tell you how I came to wreck my beautiful sports car you.
see when I made my decision to buy my "baby"- the salesman ask me how I was going to pay I said "cashie" — he was surprised when I did so.'

'But Mr Peter this means that you will need insurance before leaving the premises he said. ' Ah Mrs Angeliky we Greeks have no faith in insurance companies, I thought all they did was get rich on our money. I thought they were all thieves. Anyway, to keep him happy I did as he suggested — and thank goodness I did.'

So saying he made the sign of the Cross.

'Anyway I drove out of the showroom and headed for my factory, there were a few things I had to do before I returned home. As I rounded the corner and drove into Arnold Rd, there was Mustafa, he was washing his blue BMW. As I approached I revved the motor — Brum!Brum!, you should have seen the startled expression on his face. Then the catastrophe happened — my foot slipped off the brake becoming wedged between it and the accelerator. The car took off mounting the curb, (Mustafa jumped for his life) and sideswiped the BMW crashing straight into my neighbors Volvo.

That was the end of my "dream car", my beautiful Datsun ended up a pile of junk, impaled on the wreckage of my "next doors" Volvo. The only good thing — no one was hurt.

Afterwards I went home and I had to tell my wife. I thought that she would say, 'you stupid,' but much to my surprise her only reaction was she was glad I was not hurt.'

'Later I had to attend my cousins wedding, the women they were all in tears. I cried too, not tears of joy — *I cried for my poor car.'*

Spreading his hands expressively he said, 'that's my story Mrs Angela.'

Alexander was still thumping away on his laptop computer, eventually he finished shrugging his shoulders he said, 'well, it's quite straight forward really Angeliky, I will recommend payment of Peters claim — thank you for your assistance!'

I advised Peter of Alexander's remarks and translated the insurance statement for Peters signature, prior to leaving.

As we shook hands, Peter remarked in Greek — 'Mrs Angela make sure you get well paid, charge them six hours instead of four. The insurance companies – they have much money you know.'

I felt embarrassed, responding that he should not worry about it – my fee was quite generous!

Chapter 14

"The Man and the Stripper"

The seamy side of Melbourne exists in the infamous City of St. Kilda, an area that for many years has struggled to improve its image. Located on the shores of Hobson's Bay, it has a similar reputation to Sydney's Kings Cross, with its proliferation of strip clubs, brothels and exotic restaurants. Infamous as the "drug centre" of Melbourne — its "city fathers" have tried over the years to at least drive the "ladies of the night" underground and with the help of undercover police remove the "drug dealers" from the streets. This "entertainment zone", is contained in the precinct bounded by Fitzroy Street from the Junction to Marine Parade with Luna Park a recently renovated fun park — which dates back to the early 1900's.

It is along this quiet strip of beach front and gardens, that the addicts of Melbourne unhappily "shoot up" — some regrettably into a state of permanent oblivion.

Happily though this chapter is not about this rather depressing subject, however hopefully it will present an introduction to the next story.

Dimitri Pelagos, a red blooded Greek lad of some 25 years of age became engaged to a beautiful raven haired young lady named Sofia — but perhaps I'm getting ahead of myself.

Three months prior, he had arrived from Athens, to work in the grocery business of his Great Uncle Ari, who had the distinction of being one of the few Greek emigrants to arrive in Australia in the late 1930's, just prior to the Second World War. Uncle Ari had not entered the customary occupation of many Greeks of that time — either opening restaurants or the great Australian "fish and chips" shop (only two words of English being needed). The problem with the latter occupation being, the smell of the fish had to be acceptable to the young lady when the couple went courting if a union was ever to be contemplated. Dimitri was lucky however as he did not have to endure this difficulty — neither had the beautiful Sofia.

Upon his arrival the lucky Dimitri went straight to work at Uncle Ari's grocery in the outer Melbourne garden suburb of Balwyn. This area was settled by successful Greeks who had moved out of Richmond — for so many years the centre of the Grecian social scene.

In due course Dimitri's family arrived in Melbourne, settling nearby in Bulleen. Again it suited Uncle Ari to have the "family", running his Grecian Supermarket, people had to eat and with a hard core of Greek customers, and Dimitri's family in control, he could "retire".

Uncle Ari was lucky though, for his children had long since flown the family nest, and were happily occupied working in the family Supermarket.

It was on a day in late March, just prior to the Greek Easter late in the afternoon, that Sofia entered Uncle Aris Supermarket to be served by Dimitri.

They could not take their eyes off each other, and the romance blossomed.

It was a classic case of "love at first sight".

Prior to Easter, the Pelagos family celebrated this most holy of dates in the Greek calendar by "fasting". They were to attend the Orthodox Church in East Kew at midnight on Good Friday to witness the Ascension of Christ. The lighting of candles at the altar, aided rather explosively, by the fireworks and rockets used to celebrate the occasion as they burst in the black velvet of the night sky. It was in the midst of the celebrations that Dimitri met Sofia's family for the first time.

Uncle Ari, who had accompanied them of course knew the Pelagos family - they warmly greeted him, and were surprised that young Dimitri working in the Supermarket was friendly with Sofia.

It was later Dimitri visited Sofia's father and asked for her 'hand in marriage'.

What had they to lose, thought Pappa Nikos,- Ari was such a good boy, with a great future in Uncle Ari's Supermarket.

Sofia was 21 years of age, beautiful and available, — this was the perfect match.

Why should he object — particularly when his only daughter Sophia was wandering around with 'stars in her eyes,' talking only of Dimitri.

The date was fixed, the Greek Orthodox Church in Northcote agreed upon, and the reception venue "Gloria" at Tullamarine reserved.

It was decided that Uncle Ari's eldest son Costas, would act as "best man," his brother Peter was to be "groomsman" — his sisters Dimitra and Jenny were to act as bridesmaids.

Everything seemed perfect!

As the "big day" drew near, suits were ordered, the finishing touches made to dresses, and last but not least, Costas, who was used to Australian customs, brought up the subject of the "Bucks Night."

'What is this Bucks Night,' Dimitri asked.

'Oh don't you worry about that, it's an essentially Australian custom they assured him —

you're in Australia now and it's part of the wedding ritual.'

'Okay', he replied, 'lets go out together.'

They decided to hold Dimitri's big night on the Wednesday prior to the wedding, 'it will give you plenty of time to get over it,' said Uncle Ari shaking his head with a rye smile. 'I don't know, you young people are becoming too Australian — but you are young and you must enjoy yourselves I guess.'

Costas and Peter called as arranged on the Wednesday evening prior to the big day.

The taxi reserved by Uncle Ari called to pick up the three boys, and take them to St.Kilda where they were meeting other friends at the Savoy Hotel for dinner and a floor show.

Once on the new Eastern freeway, the leafy suburb of Balwyn soon became the outer industrial suburb of Collingwood, then they turned into Hoddle Street and down to the busy St.Kilda Junction and the start of the night's fun.

'Where in St. Kilda mate,' asked the taxi driver.

Costas replied, 'The Savoy Hotel thanks.'

'Okay we're nearly there — here's my card if I can help you later on,' replied the taxi driver with a smile on his face. 'Just call me on your mobile when you're ready to return home.'

The taxi drew up outside old stucco faced "Savoy Hotel", the neon sign flashing on and off, in pink and light blue. Ascending the steps and moving inside, they were confronted by its dark musty interior. A scantily clad waitress met them and led the way to a large table in front of a semi circular stage partially hidden by a large red velvet curtain. His eyes slowly became accustomed to its rose tinted gloom. All his male relatives were there, together with other folk associated with his and Uncle Ari's family.

The festivities had already begun, jugs of beer, bottles of wine and bottles of soft drink cluttered the table. Dimitri, the "guest of honor", was seated at its head flanked by his "best man" and groomsmen. The meal - served by one of the briefly clad "hostesses", comprised a seafood entree (from which the luckier seafood seemed to have escaped). A cremated T-Bone steak and salad followed by a large slice of Italian ice cream.

The quality of the food seemed to matter less and less, as he started to drink the potent Australian beer, encouraged by the assembled males.

Suddenly the pink gloom in which he was eating was shattered by the raucous sound announcing, 'ladies and gentlemen (there were no ladies except the waitresses) it's show time at "The Savoy". A fanfare of taped music crackled forth from the loudspeakers and the pink and blue light bulbs surrounding the stage burst into life, flashing on and off. The red velvet curtains surrounding the stage burst open and a short greasy man (clad in a shiny dinner suit that had seen better days) ran on to the stage shouting into a silver microphone.

'Welcome folks, to "show time" at the Savoy Hotel.'

Following the introduction - whatever the show did or did not contain was of little consequence — the alcohol was starting to take effect.

Dimitri was feeling as though he was looking at the scene through the walls of a glass fish bowl - into another world.

Summoned to the stage by one of the "artists" dressed as a 'school mistress, she scolded him for supposedly having peeped through a hole in the 'stage fence,' into the girls dressing room. Dimitri was way past caring when she said 'take off your belt and pull down your trousers you naughty boy.'

He removed his belt handing it to her, while at the same time she pulled down his trousers, hitting him twice on the buttocks with the leather belt.

There was a resounding, "crack, crack".

The room erupted in laughter, but there was none from Dimitri's table, who arose as one. Costas and Peter jumped on to the stage to rescue their charge. Costas grabbed the girl by the arm, taking aim at her with his clenched fist — fortunately Peter managed to deflect the blow.

In the Greek culture, this was the ultimate insult — a woman does not strike a man and certainly not their groom — of all people!

Before anything serious could occur, Costas was restrained from behind and separated from the girl by several of the guests.

The "bouncers" were outclassed, and knew it, so the Police were summoned.

Confusion reigned until the sound of a siren, heralded the arrival of the police who burst into the showroom separating the combatants. It was only then that some semblance of order was restored.

It was about 9 pm on a warm Wednesday evening, we had just finished cooking a family barbecue when the phone rang.

'Mrs Gard, are you the Greek Interpreter?' the voice asked.

'Yes, I replied, how can I help you.

'My name is Constable Bill James of St. Kilda Police, we have quite a problem.

Basically there has been an assault committed by one of your countrymen, and I'm afraid the gentleman in question speaks very little English — of course our Greek is non existent. Is it possible for you to come over to help us calm the situation?'

'Okay I replied, where is the Station situated in St. Kilda', I asked.

'We are located at the St. Kilda Road Police Complex near the Shrine — when you arrive ask, for Senior Constable Bill James.

'Thanks very much, we really appreciate your agreeing to come' he said.

'I'll be there as quickly as I can, I replied, 'it should take me about an hour.'

'Oh that's fine, he replied, they are not going anywhere.'

It was 9.30 pm in the evening and those people who were going out to dinner or a show were already there. Traffic on the Eastern freeway was light — so I made good time to Hoddle Street and then St. Kilda Road.

I parked close to the St. Kilda Police Complex, taking care to ensure I was in a signed parking area — nothing would be more embarrassing than to be "booked" by my clients. The Police Complex is a large modern building designed no doubt to take care of the criminal "goings on", at the southern end of the City of Melbourne, and the tourist precinct, of St.Kilda.

Senior Constable Bill James was easily located, and said how pleased he was to see me, as it was a Saturday night and Greek interpreters were as "scarce as hens teeth", most having other things on their mind apart from work.

He commenced, 'briefly, an assault has taken place in the Savoy Hotel St. Kilda, and we're trying to get to the bottom of exactly how it was caused. I'll take you to one of the interview rooms where we're holding them, and let you have a chat to see if you can uncover exactly what has caused the problem.

Actually they're all a bit tipsy, and of course the language problem doesn't help.'

I was shown into a large green walled windowless room — there sat Dimitri, Costas, and Peter, together with Spiro, Andrew, and Michael, looking very much the "worst for wear."

I greeted them with - 'good evening gentlemen, my name is Angeliky Gard, I'm the interpreter requested by the Police on your behalf.'

Immediately the rather somber mood in the room changed.

'Now tell me what has happened and I'll try to help you,' I commenced.

'Mrs Angeliky my name is Costas, I am Dimitri's "best man" — we took him to the Savoy Hotel in St. Kilda to celebrate his last night of "freedom" before he marries my sister Sofia. He was invited onto the stage during the show and his trousers taken down as well as being hit twice on his bottom with his belt. The girl — she was a "stripper", thought it was all a big joke. We are men Mrs Angeliky. Who does this cheap tart think she is? We will not put up with this, a woman does not do this to a man.'

I nodded and then the story started to unfold; the "best man", seeing what had occurred attempted to restrain the "stripper", fortunately no blows actually landed.

Dimitri the groom, was almost in tears — 'Sofia will never marry me when she finds out about this,' he cried.

During this long and complicated explanation, Senior Constable James sat there waiting impassively for us to finish.

I turned to him, 'Senior Constable James I have worked out what has happened. I think you are detaining these people as the result of a misunderstanding. I continued — part of their show required one member of the audience to be spanked by the stripper. There was no explanation to the party and Dimitri was assaulted by the "stripper" in no uncertain fashion — which triggered his friend's response.

Now, where is the lady in question,' I asked.

'Actually, she's in the adjoining room,' replied Senior Constable James smiling broadly.

'Okay, could you go and ask her as to whether she has suffered any actual physical harm,' I suggested.

'Alright, I will Mrs Gard, just a moment and I'll be back,' he replied leaving the room.

'Mrs Angeliky, what is happening,' they asked anxiously.

'I said I would try to help you, and this is what I'm trying to do,' I replied.

Three minutes elapsed, and a smiling Senior Constable James returned to the room.

'You're quite right Mrs Gard, the lady in question apart from getting one heck of a fright, is quite unharmed. She agreed that the whole episode has been a misunderstanding for which she is sincerely sorry, after I explained the cultural aspect.'

When I explained this to the boys, smiles broke out all around, they shook my hand thanking me profusely. The relief in the room was profound.

'Now, please go home, the whole matter is forgotten — but please ensure that a non drinker drives, said Senior Constable James. I don't want to see you lot again.'

'Thanks very much for all your assistance Angeliky, said Senior Constable James, you saved us all from a very delicate situation.'

Postscript.

A few days later my husband and I were surprised to receive an invitation to attend the wedding of Sofia and Dimitri at St. George's Orthodox Church in David Street Northcote — naturally we accepted.

On the appointed day at the time mentioned on the invitation, we arrived in David St at the only Church we could find — the Greek Church of St. Andrea which was operated by Greek Evangelists.

Goodness — whatever next, I thought. To further complicate matters a totally unknown lady waved to us, greeting us warmly trying to shepherd us inside.

I quickly realized it was the wrong Church, as no wedding was about to take place.

Surprised by the warmth of her welcome I said, 'I'm sorry — do I know you?'

'No you don't, she replied, but welcome, welcome again to St. Andreas.'

'Oh dear I don't think you understand, we are to attend a wedding at St. Georges Orthodox Church in David Street,' I replied — her face fell.

'This used to be St. George's, David Street, but it has moved further up the road,' she said pointing to her right.

Three minutes later as we arrived in front of the Church of St.George in David Street, and the heavens opened — it literally poured with rain.

So Dimitri and Sofia were married according to the grand Byzantine rites of the Greek Orthodox Church, what a lovely couple they made as they received our congratulations.

An inscription beneath the churches stained glass window read as follows —

"Erected to Glory of God and to the memory of Canon James Brown having been killed in the service of his country at Villiers Bretonneux France during the Great War of 1914 — 1918"

I couldn't help wondering what would the original reverend father of this quaint little ex Anglican Church have thought, as he stared down from his stained glass window.

"My, how things have changed — it's all Greek to me now"

"THE BEGINNING"
OF THE END

Chapter 15

"How did it all start?"

Now that you the reader, have successfully negotiated the book, I thought I'd explain the rather unusual story as to how I came to live in Australia.

I guess my side of the story starts in the early spring of 1962, in Athens Greece. I was returning home from my English class with a friend — Koolitsa. Our meeting signaled the commencement of a big change in my life. Eventually it was to entail me leaving Greece and traveling to a country on the other side of the world — Australia.

We observed the young man obviously lost, walking towards us. He addressed us in a language that I recognized as French. As there was a disappointing reaction from us he tried English, then my years of study proved useful. We discovered he was trying to find the office of Olympic Airways in Constitution Square and had become lost. Frankly it was out of our way but we were curious about him. He was polite, so we decided to walk with him and show the way.

Our new friend was most grateful, we asked was he English, to which he replied — 'no, Australian.'

Accents being accents, we understood this to mean Austrian. 'No' he said, and gave each of us a brown coin, on one side of which was a kangaroo.

Then we understood — of course he was an Australian.

Eventually we reached "Olympics" office, said our good byes, however before leaving he asked if I would like to write to him in London. I agreed, so after exchanging addresses we went our separate ways.

I didn't think much more about our meeting until about a week later, when a postcard arrived thanking us for our assistance.

Two years of letter writing followed — slowly my English improved, and so did his written Greek judging from the envelopes.

I was naturally surprised and delighted to receive a letter to say he was returning to Greece before sailing for Australia, and could we meet once again.

I was very pleased to meet him once more, for over the two years we had become firm friends.

Two months passed and another postcard arrived arranging a meeting in Constitution Square some three weeks later. Although we had written for approximately two years, my parents consented only on the condition that my older cousin Litsa accompanied us.

Our meeting was a great success. Half way through, Litsa decided she had better things to do — she apparently approved, so she departed.

We met several times over the next few days, and eventually I said a final farewell before he boarded the **"PATRIS"** in Piraeus, I thought that this will be the last time we would meet.

Imagine my surprise when a letter arrived containing a marriage proposal. My parents were thunder struck, the rest of the family was in shock. My cousin however who met and liked Keith supported me. The decision was a difficult one as in those days, it was very unusual for a young Athenian to be uprooted from Greece and resettle in a country so far away.

Australia was known to our "country people" as it was popular with migrants in those days. Athenians considered Australia to be at the other end of the earth.

What a decision I had to make. Keith had instructed me to reply to his address in Melbourne, so with the help of my cousin, I wrote to him answering neither "yes" or "no".

That gave me time to decide, and decide I did, frankly it was a case of "a deep friendship turning into love", and irrespective of what my family thought I decided to marry him.

Keith established himself, and some 11months later, a **QANTAS** air ticket arrived.

My big adventure was about to commence. In those days the journey took some 32 hours by Boeing 707, via Singapore to Sydney.

I arrived exhausted in Sydney and there was Keith to meet me. Iin those days, Melbournes Tullamarine Airport had not been built.

We were married a month later, settling into our own home in the outer Melbourne suburb of East Doncaster.

So began one of the loneliest periods of my life. Each day I sat at home practicing my English, haunting the letterbox, aching to hear the Greek language. One evening, after a fit of my tears, Keith decided the only way for me to become used to Australia and its customs was to obtain employment. With his help I did so, in the now absorbed English Scottish and Australian Bank — in those days one of the leaders in assisting migrants upon their arrival in Australia.

I was accepted as an interpreter in the Greek language, and was taught about Banking.

Now I had the best of both worlds, even better I was being paid to speak my own language.

Four years of adjustment followed during which I thoroughly enjoyed my new role.

Keith and I left each morning, returning together each evening.

Working in a bank was entirely foreign to me, however with Keith's help in explaining the system under which it operated and the friendly assistance of a young girl called "Helen", I quickly understood the work and of course enjoyed speaking my own language.

Helen and I are still in touch today.

Did I make new friends — I certainly did, both Greek and Australian.

Mary and Spiro, a young Greek couple, managed our local milk bar. Can you imagine my delight to hear my own language being spoken each night when returning home.

We became firm friends.

The Karidis children are now adult, with Mary a very proud grandmother ; the family are still our closest friends. Sadly our friend Spiro (Mary's husband) has since passed away.

As our first child (Andrew) was about to arrive, I said "goodbye" to my banking friends, content to settle back into my role as a housewife and mother — there was life after banking.

To fill the financial gap Keith undertook two other jobs on weekends, working in the Bank of Adelaide during the week, spending each Saturday morning in a travel agency while working as a salesman for a builder on Saturday and Sunday afternoons.

Two years later, our beautiful little daughter Danielle was born — our happiness was complete. In order that the children would know their father I decided to recommence work once again, this time as a "freelance interpreter".

Naturally we had to give considerable thought to the question of a "baby sitter", however this was easily solved, as our next door neighbors grandmother was known and loved by our children. They called her — "Nanna".

The years flew by and our children went their separate academic ways. Danielle to Latrobe University where she read for her Bachelor of Arts, and Andrew to Box Hill Tafe to study hospitality. Andrew departed Australia in 1998, to live and work in London, where he joined the staff of **BRITISH AIRWAYS** and successfully completed training as cabin crew member. Danielle joined the staff of **QANTAS,** following in the same occupation.

Sadly the Interpreters Club is no more, the "Godmother", Lily passed away peacefully in her sleep some two years ago while our "Nanna", instrumental in raising our children, has similarly left us.

But it was not all bad news, we have since welcomed Shane to our family, having married our daughter Danielle.

We are delighted to have such a fine young man as our son-in-law, his Italian family background further enriching our lives.

Seven years ago now, our own little "Princess" came into the world.

Cheeky our litttle "Katya Angeliky" arrived on the 28th June 2002, and more recently Lucas, Christian and baby Sara were born.

So in the beginning there were two cultures : English and Greek in our lives, now there are three.

The interpreting profession is ongoing. The Greek and Italian work is diminishing, as the post second world war migrant's children form part of our new generation. Of course they speak both languages, therefore only a few hardy souls such as I, are still assisting the barristers and doctors in the courts and hospitals.

Newcomers from Asia have settled in our land, and one day there may be another book written on this subject entitled - **"It's all Chinese to me"**.

Who knows - we must wait and see!

EULOGY

My Fathers Eulogy written by Andrew Gard and read out at his Funeral.

Dearest family,

And that's how I would like to regard you all. One family.

That's how Dad would have wanted you to feel.

My name is Andrew, Keith's son. I want to welcome you all today to celebrate the life of my Dad.

Over the last couple of days things have been very hard for both myself, my Mum, my sister Danni, Shane, my sisters kids and my fiancé Helen.

However, looking out into the sea of familiar faces, I can just hear Dad go "Kiky, why on earth are they gathering here today and looking so sad?"

Dad would not have wanted sadness. All he would have wanted was happiness, a chat and a good old cuppa tea. Tea being something he was passionate for all his life.

As some of you would know, I read a lot of books on personal development and goal setting. Books that help you to try and improve your life. One of these books is about changing your perception of a situation. I decided to use this principle and change how I see this occasion. I don't look at this as a loss, rather than a joyous celebration of his beautiful life.

Since Dads passing, I was wondering how I would describe Dads character? He was a kind, gentle person. A true to life definition of the term "English Gentlemen". Always wanting to help others. He got no better sense of joy when he helped a person over-come their "hurdles" in life.

My Dad and I were very different people yet at the same time, very similar. We have a desire to help people and we both have a good sense of what is right and what is wrong in life. Furthermore, it must be said, that in 1962, my Dad met my Mum, in a street in Athens Greece when he was trying to find the Australian Consulate. (Well, that was the story he told as to how he met my Mum, the old smoothie!)

They became pen pals and married two years later. I met my beautiful fiancé Helen in a coffee shop in London. Some things never change from one generation to the next, like Father like son.

I asked myself what things do we celebrate today that my Dad loved and people didn't know about or in fact did know about.

My Father loved and was known for :

-Dame Edna and her Business Partner Barry Humphries.

-His sense of right and wrong.

-The school he attended during his youth, Camberwell Grammar, which he was determined to get me enrolled in and subsequently succeeded. The school he adored attending and cherished talking about right up until he left us.

-His love of scuba-diving when he was younger.

-The only person I have ever known to have broken Greek Airport Security when he flashed his business card at one of the Airport Personnel and was ushered airside to meet a group of Australians he was taking around Europe. True story.

-Helping others with any problems whether it be the neighbours children's homework or teaching his beloved grand-kids the times table.

-His bewilderment as too why I would want to watch a movie so many times on DVD when I had seen it in the cinema.

-His continued ability to loose his wallet on a daily basis. When he asked for it last week in hospital, Mum pulled it out of her bag. I then told him it was in Mums bag all of these years for which he just laughed.

-His joy of having Australian Residency and keeping his British Citizenship.

-His displeasure for me not having a shave on a daily basis.

-Up until his retirement, his love of the travel industry and his continued love of travel after he retired.

-The television series "Dads Army".

-His well known love of tea. (No matter what the outside temperature!)

-Opening the doors of a little known country at the time called Albania to Australian Tourists.

-His love of North Face Jackets which he asked me to buy when I went to China.

-Unusually enough, his love of "The Lord of the Rings" feature films that he went to every Boxing Day when they were released over three consecutive years.

-His love of St Andrews Market in Warrandyte that he went to fortnightly with my Mum and our Thea Mary Karadis.

-The fact that he tried to pioneer the introduction of the edible potato cup years ago which I believe to this day, was a concept ahead of its time.

-And finally his love for my Mother (whom he was married to for 48 beautiful years) and the love he had for myself, Helen my fiancé, Danni, my sister, Shane her husband and his four beautiful grandchildren, Katya, Luke, Christian and Sara.

That summed up my Dad Keith.

So as I stand here in front of you today (fully shaved Dad after burning out the motor of my electric razor for you) I would ask that people not say we are sorry for your loss. I do not want to hear that we send our condolences.

I respectfully ask that we all change our thinking in that we alter our perception and celebrate together that God gave us Keith, my Dad, who was part of this life for 75 glorious years.

As you leave today and go back to your families and your lives, you can all continue the celebration of my Dads life. It's something that is very simple and requires no effort.

All it involves is to love your family, be kind to people you deal with in your lives, be pleasant with people that annoy you and do a good deed if you can, every day.

That's how Dad will be remembered and will never be forgotten. That's what he would have wanted. He wouldn't have it any other way.

My final words to Dad as he was leaving us was "thank you for installing the moral values, standards and ideals to be a good person. I will keep them and follow them for the rest of my life". To continue having that kind of attitude in life, would be the best way to honour his life and legacy.

God bless Dad. Safe journey and happy landings as he told me every time I arrive back from a trip for the last 16 years.

You will be missed but everywhere I look, your presence and beautiful smile, will always shine and never be far away.

Thank-you all for your time and God Bless you all. We thank you for attending and supporting us today. That to me is what family is all about.

Keith Gard was raised in both London and Melbourne Australia. Co-written with his Wife Angeliky, this book was 10 years in the making and is a testament to the tribulations and "trials" of life in the field of Legal Interpreting.

Keith passed away in January 2014 but his legacy will live on through the love his family will always have of him and the book that he so passionately loved working on.

He is survived by his wife Angeliky, his two children Andrew and Danielle, their respective partners and his four beautiful grandchildren.

Printed in the United States
by Baker & Taylor Publisher Services